Hearts of Gold

Miss Beaumont's Companion

GRACE HITCHCOCK

Published by Valmont House Publishers

GraceHitchcock.com

Names: Hitchcock, Grace, author.

Title: Miss Beaumont's Companion / Grace Hitchcock

Other Titles: miss beaumont's companion

Identifiers: 978-1-970675-05-4 Paperback

Subjects: Christian Romantic fiction

All scripture quotations, unless otherwise noted, are taken from the King James Version of the Bible.

Cover design by *Valmont House Publishers*

Editor Ellen Tarver

Author is represented by The Steve Laube Agency

More From Grace Hitchcock:

Aprons and Veils Series:
The Finding of Miss Fairfield
The Pursuit of Miss Parish
The Enchanting of Miss Elliot
The Vanishing of Miss Victoria
The Courting of Miss Cady
The Making of Miss Matthews

Best Laid Plans Series:
To Catch a Coronet
To Kiss a Knight
To Win a Wager

American Royalty Series:
My Dear Miss Dupré
Her Darling Mr. Day
His Delightful Lady Delia

Heiresses of Adventure Series:
Miss Blaire in Blackwell's Island
Miss Wylde in the White City

Novellas:

Hearts of Gold, A Historical Romance Collection

"The Widow of St. Charles Avenue" in Second Chance Brides Collection

To my Dakota,
a true man with a heart
of gold

Look at the birds of the air; they do not sow or reap or store away in barns, and yet your heavenly Father feeds them. Are you not much more valuable than they?

MATTHEW 6:26 NIV

CHAPTER ONE

aton Rouge, Louisiana,
October 1892

"BREATHE. JUST BREATHE," Aria whispered as she adjusted the ribbons on her mask, ensuring that her identity was kept safe.

"Now, you know what you must do, Miss St. Angelo," her employer reminded her as the carriage wheels crunched to a halt on the gravel drive in front of the governor's mansion.

"Smile, dance, and make small talk with the politicians." She smoothed the royal-blue replica of a Marie Antoinette gown she was wearing.

"*And* get an introduction with Byron Roderick to secure a call," Mr. Beaumont reiterated. "My daughter is going to pay for disappearing with her aunt this afternoon. Mildred knows how much I need her at Governor Foster's masquerade ball to meet the state senator's son." He turned his dark eyes to her. "If I weren't so concerned about making an inferior impression by being tardy, I would have dragged her back by her coiffure," he growled. "It's imperative for my political future that no one discovers you're not Mildred. If you ruin this night for me, I needn't remind you of the repercussions to your future."

"Yes, sir," she whispered. As the granddaughter of reduced aristocratic Italian immigrants, her options for a respectable living were limited. Even though she cringed at the idea of pretending to be her employer's daughter at the ball, she knew that if she didn't execute this task, Mr. Beaumont would be true to his word and throw her out. She also knew that his daughter could do little to stop it, especially since she was the one who created this ridiculous situation in the first place by sneaking off without a word.

His eyes narrowed at her powdered skin, disguising her olive complexion, and pile of powdered hair. "Straighten your wig. One glimpse of your black hair and the facade is shattered. You're wearing heeled shoes, I hope?"

She nodded. *It's only a little fib. Who will it hurt?* With one hand steadying her wig, Aria gathered her skirts in the other and descended the carriage, stepping into Mildred Beaumont's identity as she crossed the threshold of the governor's mansion. The butler at the door, dressed in Revolutionary-era breeches, coat, and tricornered hat, bowed and removed her cloak. She gave him a small smile of thanks before falling into step behind Mr. Beaumont. At her employer's pointed stare, she realized her blunder and awkwardly threaded her arm through his as if they were truly father and daughter.

Her breath caught at the sight of the

masked ladies and gentlemen on the ballroom floor, whirling in the light of hundreds of candles flickering in the chandeliers, candelabras, and sconces. Some of the gentlemen around her wore pirate trappings, animal heads, and bandit costumes, but most of them merely wore masks. *Probably just to appease their wives,* she surmised by the sullen press of their lips. There were a few women in bold regency gowns, some in Colonial attire, and far too many Marie Antoinette costumes roaming about. She felt a giggle rise within, knowing how furious Mildred would be to know her costly, "unique" costume was donned by at least nine other women. Her exquisite gown had become positively average.

Mr. Beaumont snatched an appetizer from the silver tray of a passing maskless footman who was dressed in the same breeches attire as the butler to distinguish himself from the guests. She reached for a miniature crab cake, but Mr. Beaumont squeezed her elbow.

"Too smelly," he muttered under his

breath as she reluctantly drew back her hand. "Smile brightly and be engaging."

He pulled her toward a group and introduced her to diplomat after senator after representative, making her head dance. She bravely made small talk until her stomach rumbled. Her eyes grew wide as she discreetly pushed a hand against her corset stays and silently begged for the tête-à-tête to end when her stomach rumbled again. Blushing, she quietly excused herself to find the banquet table.

She scanned the room for food but, feeling eyes upon her, turned to see the distinct flash of white-blond hair belonging to Mildred's former beau, Joel Branson, who was staring at her from across the room with his soon-to-be fiancée draped over his arm and the banquet room behind them. Her heart stopped as recognition lit his eyes. She touched the corner of her mask. *Millie must've told him what her gown looked like before he broke their relationship off to be with Fiona,* she thought as he leaned down and whispered into Fiona's ear. Sensing he was about to seek her out, Aria settled for an Italian pastry from one of the dessert tables. Then, before he could make his way through the ballroom, she ducked into an unlit hallway for a bit of privacy. *No wonder Millie decided to escape tonight if she knew that horrid man would be here.* She stepped into the dark recesses of the hallway and stole a bite of cannoli.

BYRON RODERICK HATED the politics behind attending a masquerade ball, but as the son of an influential state senator, he smiled and supported his father as expected. After all, everyone knew he was being groomed for the office himself.

"Don't you think so, Mr. Roderick?" the overeager mother questioned.

"Uh, yes," he replied as he tugged the coat of his costume, hoping his response was the correct answer to the question he hadn't heard. He had attempted to be Paul Revere, but to his amusement, he matched the servants, which was why he'd discarded his mask and put on his wire-rimmed spectacles so he could at least be recognized. But now with the mothers circling him with their single daughters in tow, he began to wish he had left it in place.

Before the current predator could ask yet another question, he excused himself and headed for the dark hallway. *I'll probably pay for that later.* He sighed, rubbing his hands over his eyes as he stepped on something soft and heard a muffled squeal. Startled, he looked down into a pair of dark eyes behind an elaborate Venetian mask. The petite lady, dressed in a cloud of royal blue, stumbled away from his boot and back into a column.

"I'm so sorry, miss!" He grabbed her by the elbows to steady her, spying a half-eaten cannoli in her hand.

"No, it's my fault." She held her hand over her mouth as she talked around a mouthful of pastry, quickly swallowing. "How could you expect to see me in such a dark space?"

"Were you hiding from someone too?" he asked, adjusting his glasses.

Laughing, she nodded and lifted up her dessert plate. "I haven't had a bite to eat all evening. I was trying to consume this before my, uh, father finds that last politician he wants me to meet. A Mr. Byron Roderick. Have you met him? He's probably just another overweight, red-faced man twenty years my senior." She glanced at the pastry, obviously wishing to finish the treat.

"Ah, I believe I might know whom you are speaking of." He struggled to swallow back his amusement at her candor as he motioned for her to continue eating. "Tell me, what would you rather be doing on a night like this?"

She leaned forward in a conspiratorial whisper. "Honestly? I'd like to finish my book tonight, but my father insisted I go husband hunting instead."

Biting back his laughter at this refreshing young lady, Byron smiled, and with a flourished bow, introduced himself as she took another mouthful.

ARIA CHOKED ON HER PASTRY, and the man dressed in the servant's costume gently slapped her on the back. "I am so sorry," she croaked into her napkin. "I thought you were one of the staff as you weren't wearing a mask! I never would have spoken so outrageously if I thought—"

He laughed, taking her empty plate and setting it aside on a vacant chair. "But then I wouldn't have gotten to know you quite so well, now would I, Miss. . . ?"

"Beaumont." She dipped into a curtsy. "Millie, I mean, Mildred Beaumont," she added in a fuller southern lilt, as Millie might. *How do I fix this? If Mr. Beaumont finds out I've insulted the very man he wishes Millie to marry, he will relieve me of my position.* "So, who were you attempting to run away from?" She took in his towering height, broad shoulders, and chestnut hair and gave him what she hoped was a captivating smile.

"A horde of mothers and their single daughters." He peeked around the column. "But as they seem to be occupied at present, it may be safe to reappear." He turned back to her, extending his hand. "Miss Beaumont, would you do this lawyer the honor of being his partner for the next dance even if he isn't a politician twenty years your senior?"

Feeling her cheeks burn, she let out a shaky laugh as she surrendered her hand to him and then realized that the next dance was still a few minutes away from beginning. Yet, he didn't seem to mind having her hand threaded through his arm.

"So, tell me. What do you like to read when you're not husband hunting?"

She stumbled to answer as Millie would. All she could remember Millie reading was the latest fashion magazines, but as that hardly seemed like a good enough answer to incline his interest to calling, she answered truthfully as herself. "Charles Dickens. My favorite of his works is *Little Dorrit*."

Mr. Roderick's brows rose, and he began another line of questioning that sent her scrambling for Millie-approved answers when the music concluded. *Thank goodness the dance is starting.* She held back a sigh, grateful to be free from fibbing for the moment. Over the next few minutes, she learned that he was an excellent dance partner, and as she dearly loved a waltz but rarely had the opportunity to dance, she allowed herself to get lost in the dips of the violins as he guided her about the room and she hummed along with the music.

"You sing," he stated rather than asked.

She nodded. "My mother is quite accomplished and taught me as a small child."

"Is Mrs. Beaumont with you this evening?"

Realizing her blunder a little too late, she cringed. "I mean *was* accomplished. She still seems so near," she lied, thinking how her perfectly healthy mother was living with their large family in the French Quarter where her father worked as a clerk.

"I'm so sorry to hear that," he replied, mistaking her expression for grief.

Aria dipped her head as she imagined Mildred might. "Thank you."

"May I cut in?"

Aria snapped her head up to find her gaze met by Joel Branson's.

Mr. Roderick bowed to her, giving her

an apologetic smile as Joel stepped in, placing his hand about her waist. "You've become quite slim," he commented.

Aria's eyes flared at the inappropriate comment, but she knew if she answered, he would guess her secret.

"I suppose you're still angry with me for breaking things off with you and forming an attachment with Fiona?"

Not daring to reply, she shook her head.

"Then why have you been avoiding me?" Joel whispered. "I know you want me. You know I only started courting Fiona to show your father I was serious about the dowry's importance. I still love you. All you have to do is convince your father to give you a larger dowry, enough to tempt me away from Fiona's fortune."

She kept her gaze averted as anger rippled through her veins. *Is this what poor Millie had to endure? She said Joel was manipulative, but to use her love for him as a means to obtain wealth? Despicable.*

"Do you really want to take a chance with one of these ancient bachelors or widowers when you know I would adore you as my wife?" He twirled her in his arms as the final notes played. "You have one month before I ask for Fiona's hand. Think carefully, my dear," he whispered as he bowed and left her on the floor, alone.

Mr. Roderick returned to her side, concerned lines etched between his eyes as he escorted her off the floor. "I'm sorry. If I had known you didn't wish to dance with him, I wouldn't have allowed him to cut in."

She shook her head and tried to return a smile to her face. "I didn't know I had let my feelings show so. I was a little uncomfortable, yes, but thankfully it was only for a moment." *Flirt with him.* She turned a sparkling smile up to him. "And now I'm back with you and perfectly content."

He stopped by the refreshment table. Handing her a glass of lemonade, he said, "This may be a bit presumptuous, but I would love to see you again. Would you allow me to call on you tomorrow?"

Her heart skipped a beat at the thought of spending more time with him, but then sank as she realized he wouldn't actually be calling on *her*. Mr. Roderick would be seeing Millie, the youngest daughter of a politician. . .someone of status, not a poor immigrant with weak ties to Italian royalty. She took a quick sip and gave him a bold wink. “As long as it doesn’t interfere with my reading, that would be marvelous.”

CHAPTER TWO

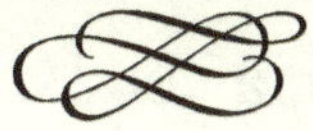

At breakfast the next morning, Mildred thrust back her chair and stood with such force it nearly toppled over. "I shouldn't be surprised anymore at the lengths you will go to protect your career, Father, but"—she turned her fiery gaze on Aria—"I cannot believe *you* would go along with his scheming."

Ignoring her protests, Mr. Beaumont picked up his newspaper and snapped it open. "Nonetheless, I expect you to receive Mr. Roderick this morning and to be not only cordial, but *interested*. And, as I said, Miss St. Angelo had no choice in the matter."

"One *always* has a choice." Mildred threw down her napkin and stormed out of the room in a flurry of skirts.

Mr. Beaumont looked up from his paper to Aria and raised his brows. "Well, what are you waiting for? Go to her."

With a sigh, Aria set aside her nearly untouched breakfast and, with a rumbling stomach, followed her charge to the parlor. Mildred sat with her feet curled under her, viciously flipping through the latest edition of *Harper's Bazaar*.

"Millie," Aria began softly, crossing the room and touching a hand to Millie's puffed sleeve, "I'm sorry I had to pretend to be you last night, but my position was in jeopardy if I refused your father." She cracked a smile. "And I have to admit that I did think that if you had thought of this plan instead of your father, you would've done it in an instant."

Millie set aside her magazine and rubbed her face, a soft laugh bubbling from her lips. "You are quite right." She dropped her hands and met Aria's gaze. "I'm sorry I was cross when I should be thanking you for stepping into my shoes and sparing me from being humiliated." She bit her lip and asked softly, "Did you see him?"

Aria fidgeted with her deep cuffs of ivory lace. "He cut in while I was dancing with Mr. Roderick and tried to speak with me, or rather you, on a delicate matter."

"He did?" Hope filled her voice as she swept her feet off the settee. She tossed her long, flowing caftan behind her velvet skirts and made her way to the window in true Mildred theatrical fashion. "Did he apologize? Is he releasing Fiona from their understanding?"

Aria's fingers traced the simple coral beads around her neck, and she slowly shook her head. "He spoke to me about your dowry. He acted as if that was the only impediment."

"It is." Millie's shoulders drooped with her voice. "Father refused to give him a dime more. If only Joel had more connections, Father wouldn't blink at a larger amount. When my sisters were courted by key politicians, Father offered them more.

He didn't even wait to be asked, Aria. And now that I am asking, he refuses."

"If money is all that is keeping you two apart, you're lucky to be rid of him," she replied softly, stroking Millie's arm.

Millie pressed her palm to her chest. "My head realizes this, but my heart. . .loves him."

Aria draped her arm about her friend's shoulders. "They say that time helps heal all wounds."

"We are nearing twenty-two years of age and are practically old maids! We don't have time for wounds to heal. Besides, this is a wound that need not be if only Father would yield and increase my dowry by a few thousand dollars." Her brows furrowed as she planted her hands on her hips. "If Mother were here, she would talk some reason into him."

"I know, but another way to heal quickly is by meeting a very handsome man. When you see him today, you will forget all about Joel Branson," Aria said, grinning.

"Handsome?" A hint of a smile appeared on Millie's pouting lips. "What kind of man is he? Please tell me he is not stiff and dull like every other suitor Father has brought to my door."

"Far from it. You're fortunate to have such a viable option in the place of Mr. Branson. I quite enjoyed my conversation with Mr. Roderick, who seems kindhearted and enjoys a laugh." She smiled, thinking of the merriment she'd spotted in the corners of his mouth. *If only he were calling on me instead of you.* Her smile froze. She could not afford such thoughts. "Now, I know you don't care much for spectacles on a man, but on him. . ." Aria's voice drifted off as she lost herself in the dream of last night. *Stop it! He's meant for Millie.*

"He wears spectacles?" Millie wrinkled her nose.

"Honestly, I think they only add to his handsomeness," she murmured as she heard gravel crunching under wheels. She peeked through the curtain to see Mr. Roderick step down from the carriage, and her heart picked up speed with every stride he took toward the front door.

"Hello? Aria, I asked you what we should

talk about." Millie tapped her on the shoulder, breaking her reverie.

The butler appeared at the door and, bowing, announced, "Mr. Byron Roderick to see you, Miss Beaumont."

"*Already?*" Millie nearly squeaked.

"Show him to the parlor and offer him some refreshments, Newton," Aria instructed. She turned to pat down Millie's golden hair, pulling a single curl over her shoulder.

Millie inhaled through her teeth with a moan. "Why didn't you wake me sooner this morning to prepare me? How am I to keep up the charade if you haven't even told me what you two spoke about? He will know that I'm not the masked lady from last night. Quick, give me a topic!"

"Books," Aria replied, straightening Millie's brooch.

"Well, that is no help whatsoever." She rolled her eyes and peered into the looking glass above the mantel, giving her cheeks a generous pinch.

"I'm sorry to rush away, but I better take my leave of you for fear he may recognize me," Aria said as she cracked open the door and glanced down the hallway to ensure she wouldn't be spotted.

"Oh no you don't." Millie whirled to face Aria. "You cannot give me little to no notice that I have a caller and then run off moments before he appears. How could you throw me to the wolves like that?"

"Mr. Roderick is hardly a wolf. Mr. Beaumont informed me last night that while the memory of me is fresh in Mr. Roderick's mind, he must only see and hear you on his first call. Tomorrow he can see me after you have convinced him that it was you he met last night and not me."

"But the topics!" Millie grasped her by the arm, halting her flight. "What books?"

"You'll be fine. Just speak of the classics and ask him about his work."

"His work? You know how much I hate the political realm," she muttered.

"He is a lawyer," Aria returned, slipping into the hallway.

"See?" Millie hissed after her. "I didn't even know that! This mission is doomed. Please don't leave me," she begged.

"I'm sorry. You know I have to listen to your father." Aria gave her a smile of encouragement. "Besides, you've always wanted to be an actress, so pretend you are on the stage and give the performance of your life."

Mildred exhaled and dropped her shoulders. "I suppose that any great actress must be ready to perform even if she has no lines to read from."

"That's the spirit." Aria grinned and quietly retrieved her shawl. She made her way out to the back gardens, hoping the blossoms would keep her mind preoccupied.

She could not allow herself to think of his hazel eyes, or to remember how it felt to dance in his arms. Plucking an orange-and-yellow lantana, she inhaled its sweet scent and thought of how refreshing it had been conversing with Mr. Roderick as an equal. She tucked the flower into her low coiffure and sighed, reaching for a pink camellia. It had been so long since someone from Millie's set had treated her as anything other than a servant. As a lady's companion, she had a foot in both worlds. She wasn't part of the downstairs staff, and yet she wasn't considered a member of the family. She was paid to be a friend and chaperone.

Hearing voices, she paused in gathering her bouquet to silence the crunch of the leaves underfoot and listened. She gazed through the evergreen hedge that led to the side garden and found Mr. Roderick conversing with Mildred on one of the benches. The sunlight fell on Mildred's locks, bathing her in a heavenly glow, but judging from the look on his face and the angle of his brows, she felt Byron Roderick appeared less animated than he'd been with her last night. *I wonder if he can tell that Millie isn't me? I was so covered in that wig, mask, and powder that it speaks of his character that he should ask to call on a woman who may have been hiding her flaws.* She prayed he would not suspect Millie.

Watching them converse, she again found herself wishing she could be in Millie's pretty shoes as she was last night, but at the thought of her large family who would go without if she lost her position, she again shook her head, attempting to dispel any thought of Byron. *He must be Mr. Roderick to me.* Though they had only met last night, she felt herself inexplicably drawn to him. She would not risk the stability of her family or her brother's future tuition funds for the sake of one man's handsome eyes.

Her stomach flipped as he bent down to bid Millie farewell and kissed her on the hand, an action that disturbed Aria more than it should. She turned away, unable to witness him falling in love with her pretty charge. Aria slowly yanked away the petals from a camellia as she ambled back inside and away from the couple. Depositing half of the bouquet in a large vase, she kept the rest for arranging in Mildred's hair. Turning the corner of the hallway, she strolled face-first into a broad chest, knocking her flowers to the floor.

Hands reached out to steady her shoulders, and she found herself once again face-to-face with Byron Roderick. She dropped her gaze, praying he would not recognize her. "I am so sorry, sir," she mumbled, stepping away from his touch as she bent to retrieve her flowers.

He beat her to them and handed the colorful bunch back to her and straightened his hat. "The fault is mine," he assured her. "Are you quite well?"

She nodded and risked a glance through her lashes up at him as she accepted the flowers and met his eyes, her heart hammering. "Please excuse me," she whispered and darted upstairs. He had not recognized her.

BYRON TUGGED his hat over his eyes and hunched his shoulders against the autumn chill as he marched back to his law practice. Something wasn't right about Mildred Beaumont. The spark he witnessed in her last night no longer lit her dark eyes, which seemed less radiant in the daylight. He shook his head at the uncharitable thought. *It was most likely the candlelight that enchanted me rather than her eyes. That and the fact she was the only woman who didn't throw herself into my arms all night.* He had secured another call with her for the following afternoon, but if it went anything like today, he wasn't sure if he would continue his pursuit.

He let himself in through the side door, nodding to his associates as he made his way to the back of the office to his private room. *She was most likely nervous. . .but last night, she was so full of confidence and genuineness. Today, she seemed like she was reading from a script and was afraid of reading a line incorrectly.*

Byron shrugged out of his coat, sank down at his desk, and tried to focus on the day's work. He shifted through a handful of files of potential clients seeking legal representation, eager to select his next couple of cases. His glance fell on a pro bono case of a young family of Irish immigrants, and he flipped through the file.

His father didn't approve of this less glamorous aspect of his work, but Byron relished helping the working man, even if it didn't pay as well as the gentlemen or parvenus cases brought to the law firm. Almost every Sunday over dinner, the elder Mr. Roderick tried to convince Byron that he could do so much more for the people in the political realm, but Byron loved the hands-on work of being a guardian angel to someone who felt that all hope was lost. He felt it was his calling to come to the aid of the less fortunate ones in society: the widows, the orphans, the poor, and those without a voice. One day, he hoped to have his own practice and dedicate more of his cases to the lower class. Until then, he could not allow this Irish family to be taken advantage of by those who knew better. Adjusting his glasses, he got to work.

CHAPTER THREE

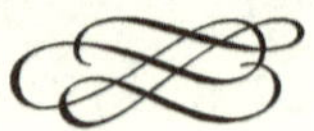

Aria stayed a few paces behind the couple and remained silent. Mr. Beaumont strictly forbade her from getting too involved, for he didn't want her to become a distraction. She was accompanying Millie and Mr. Roderick on their walk by the river to chaperone only. After spending the entire morning instructing Millie on how to keep Mr. Roderick's interest, she couldn't help but smile with approval as Millie gave all the proper responses. Yet Aria sensed the theatricality behind them and hoped Mr. Roderick didn't think her charge insincere. It would take a lot more than a handsome face to make Millie forget Joel Branson.

She shifted her reticule to the other arm. The weight of the new novel she had bought for her little brother called to her, but she knew it would be a while before they reached the coffeehouse and she could finally indulge in the book. Mildred was too fond of the river walk to hurry. To take her mind off her anticipation of reading Arthur Conan Doyle's book, Aria brought her attention back to the couple ahead of her.

Mr. Roderick commented on Millie's singing ability, and Millie gave a nervous laugh. She looked over her shoulder at Aria, her widening eyes silently begging for help.

"I would love to hear you sing sometime, Miss Beaumont," he continued.

Aria threaded her arm through Millie's, rescuing her. "Miss Beaumont shouldn't be singing anytime soon." She turned her gaze to her friend. "I'm sure your father wishes you to rest your voice after your cold last week," she added, which wasn't entirely a falsehood.

Millie's smile brightened. "Oh yes, he

told me he wants me to sing at Mrs. Foster's musicale in two weeks and wishes for me to sound my best."

"He did?" Aria's jaw dropped. *What is he thinking?*

Mildred gave her a furtive wink. "Yes! Of course he did."

Aria hid her grimace behind a gritted smile. *Why are you adding to the lie?* Mildred could carry a tune, but she was no songbird, and no amount of practicing would change that in two short weeks. "Forgive me. How could I have forgotten when I've heard you practice your piece about a dozen times." *A dozen times in two years.*

Mr. Roderick's gaze met hers, and she quickly broke their connection before he could recognize her. "Oh! I see that taffy cart you like so much, Miss Beaumont. I'll get us some chocolate taffy sticks." She hurried away so not to bring any more attention to herself than necessary.

OUT OF THE corner of his eye, Byron noticed Miss St. Angelo watching him and Miss Beaumont from three tables down. She sat near the front of the coffeehouse, appearing to enjoy her steaming café au lait and vanilla crème brûlée as she silently giggled into the pages of her novel whenever Mildred came up for air in her long-winded narratives, allowing him a rare moment to inject a sentence before she began her endless chatter again.

"Why, there's Fanny Branson!" Mildred slipped from her chair. "If you'll excuse me for one moment, I need to speak with her."

Byron rose, dropping his napkin in his haste, but she was already halfway across the room before he could reply.

Miss St. Angelo caught her arm in passing, whispering, "Are you sure that is wise?"

"Of course." Miss Beaumont scowled. "I'll return in a minute."

Byron stifled a sigh of relief for a moment's respite and turned his attention to Miss Beaumont's companion who, returning to her novel, took a generous spoonful of her vanilla custard. He stepped over to her table and tilting his head, read the spine. *"The Adventures of Sherlock Holmes,* eh?"

She lurched, dropping her spoon into her lap. "Blast," she murmured, and wiped her napkin over the stain on her gray frock.

"I'm sorry I startled you." Heat suffused Byron's face as he stood, helpless to repair the situation.

She waved a dismissive hand. "It matters not. No one will notice, and I shall work the stain away when we return."

His gaze fell on the considerable smear on her skirt, and remorse smote him. "So." He cleared his throat and glanced over toward Miss Beaumont, who was deep into her conversation with Miss Branson. "You enjoy mysteries?"

She smiled, setting her book on the table. "Not usually, but I know that if I gift this to my younger brother, my mama will ask me about its content to ensure that it is proper and I can't rightly say it is when I haven't read it." She tapped the cover. "My hope is that my brother will take to reading for his adventures again rather than finding mischief with his questionable friends. He's been longing to attend Louisiana State University since he was a small boy, but now I fear his rough companions will discourage him from seeking higher education." She shook her head and smiled at him as she rose. "I'm sorry. I'm rambling. I should see if Miss Beaumont needs me." She emitted a soft laugh. "So, if you'll excuse me. . ."

Her laugh rippled in his mind. He looked from her to Miss Beaumont and then back to Miss St. Angelo. An uncomfortable lump formed in his chest. *Why does the companion remind me more of the masked lady than Miss Beaumont does?* Byron studied the curve of Miss Beaumont's lips and the way she carried herself. The longer he stared at her, the more he came to suspect that something was amiss. *Why would Miss St. Angelo pretend to be Miss Beaumont?* But, looking at Miss St. Angelo's olive complexion, he shook his head, dispelling the foolish thought.

ARIA PERCHED on the edge of Millie's four-poster bed as the maid brushed Millie's hair, readying her for bed. "So, after spending the afternoon with Mr. Roderick, what do you think?"

"That's all for tonight, Louise." Millie waved the maid off and set to plaiting her own hair. When Louise closed the door behind her, Millie sighed. "I'd rather not risk Louise repeating our conversation to Father. I think Roderick is nice enough, but really, Aria, how could you think that he could ever compare to Joel Branson?"

Because Byron Roderick is twice the man Branson will ever become, not to mention he is kind and considerate. Aria bit back her reply. "I thought you would find him handsome and his company enjoyable."

"I didn't say he wasn't handsome." Millie finished her braid with a red silk ribbon to match her dressing robe. "And while he's not your typical politician's son, I found him quite lackluster. I as much as told Fanny Branson that so she would relay it to her brother, but the girl is practically voting for Fiona." She shook her head and tossed her braid over her shoulder, scowling. "I thought we were friends."

Aria rolled her eyes and laughed. "I can't believe you told her that! Did you forget I was merely yards away during your outing? You barely allowed the poor man to get a word in edgewise. How could you possibly think Mr. Roderick is boring if he didn't even get the chance to speak?"

Millie smirked. "Well, maybe I did monopolize the conversation. But I think you should know that I only plan to let him to court me until I can figure out how to convince Father to increase my dowry to make a marriage with Joel possible."

Aria's heart lurched. *Mr. Roderick doesn't deserve to be anyone's second choice.* "And if your father doesn't concede, will you keep stringing Mr. Roderick along?"

With a dramatic sigh, Millie flopped onto the bed, jostling Aria. "If I can't have Joel Branson for my husband, then I suppose Mr. Roderick will have to do."

CHAPTER FOUR

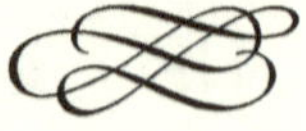

With her train ticket tucked in her reticule, Aria boarded the train for New Orleans, ready for a break from Millie's courtship. While Millie allowed Mr. Roderick to keep calling and seemed to enjoy his company, Aria knew Millie's heart wasn't in it. She still hoped against all to return to Mr. Branson's arms. After a painful two weeks of watching Mr. Roderick court Millie, Aria was more than grateful when Millie announced she was spending the weekend with a friend from school and that Aria could have a couple of days off to visit her family in New Orleans if she wished.

And she did wish it, for she had begun to long for the moments when Mr. Roderick would inevitability turn to her during his calls for their daily, brief conversations when Millie grew distracted. She drank in her stolen moments with him, knowing he would never belong to her, but with each passing week, she grew more and more tempted to break her silence. Yet she feared if she did indeed speak the truth about the night they met, she would not only lose her position but also Byron's friendship for her deception. Again and again, she resigned herself to being Millie's shadow. Even if Byron could forgive her for masquerading as Millie, he would most certainly never consider Aria for his wife when he could have the American heiress with all the political privileges that would come with such a union. Aria's heritage would bring him nothing but strife. She sighed. A little distance would do her good.

With her carpetbag tucked by her feet, Aria settled back into the tufted seats of the train, eager to see her family, whom she missed terribly. It had been far too long, and after an exhausting week of running after Millie and her endless trips to the shops and her portrait-sitting with the famous photographer Andrew Lytle, Aria looked forward to her book, or rather Millie's book. Mr. Roderick had given Millie a copy of a classic with plans to discuss it with her at a later date, but Millie, having no interest in *The Scarlet Letter*, gave the book to Aria to study and to tell her about it later.

Aria was deep into the pages of her book and sucking on a hard candy when she heard a throat clearing above her. Expecting the conductor, she reluctantly paused, marked her place in her book with a candy wrapper, and dug around her reticule for her ticket before looking up. She snapped her book shut and gasped, nearly choking on her sweet. "Mr. Roderick! What are you doing here?" She worked the question around the lump of candy, immediately wishing she hadn't indulged in a piece from the little bag she had brought for her brother and sisters. *How do I get rid of this?* she thought frantically, as she was still a good twenty minutes from it dissolving.

Why am I always eating when he catches me unawares?

"I have business in New Orleans." His smile widened. "Are you visiting your family?"

"Why, yes." She blinked, surprised that he remembered. "But what are you doing back here? Why aren't you in first class?"

"I always travel coach when alone. There's no need for me to take first."

"No need?" *If I had the option, I would always take first.* Forgetting herself, she almost chuckled, but the candy in her mouth stopped any expression of mirth. *Time for desperate measures.* Thinking quickly, she knocked her book from her lap. When he bent down to retrieve it as she knew he would, she quickly disposed of the candy into her handkerchief and stuffed it behind her. Smiling up at him, she uttered her thanks when he returned her book. "Why, how clumsy of me. *Grazie.*"

His hazel eyes sparked at her Italian, and she blushed. She was usually so careful not to slip into the comfortable language while away from home, but he unnerved her in the best of ways.

Spying the title, his brows rose. "*The Scarlet Letter*? Did Miss Beaumont finish it already?"

Not wanting to lie, Aria dusted the book cover and slowly replied, "No. Miss Beaumont graciously allowed me to take it with me to read. We are going to discuss its contents at great length later." *There, that wasn't a lie.*

"Are you enjoying it as much as *Sherlock*?" he asked, his eyes shining behind his polished glasses.

She gestured to the seat across from her. "Well, if you aren't traveling with anyone, why don't you take a seat and I'll tell you." She knew she probably shouldn't offer, but at this point in their conversation, it seemed rather rude not to invite him to sit down. Although she had to admit, it wasn't just courtesy that prompted her to offer him the empty seat.

Aria was instantly drawn into their conversation, and when the conductor announced they were pulling into New

Orleans Union Station, she looked out the window and was shocked to find herself in the city already. She reluctantly packed the book into her satchel and rose to leave, but Byron immediately relieved her of her burden and gestured for her to precede him off the train.

He walked with her outside and paused, checking his pocket watch before clicking it shut as if he too was surprised at how fast their journey seemed. "Is anyone meeting you?" he asked, looking up and down the platform.

A rare breeze cooled her hot cheeks from the stifling train car and their riveting conversation. "No, I never let them know when I'm coming, as Millie almost never plans ahead," she explained as they descended the platform steps to the busy street.

"Oh, well, I'll hail a carriage for you then." He started to raise his arm.

She quickly reached out and grasped his sleeve before he signaled a driver. "Please don't concern yourself with a carriage for me. I'm not far from my parents' home. It's only thirty minutes on foot and I could use the walk. Miss Beaumont usually isn't one for long walks, so I quite enjoy taking in the city on foot."

"Then you must allow me to see you home." He extended his arm to her. "I can't have you wandering off on your own."

Mr. Beaumont would be livid if we were seen together. "It's really not necessary," she reassured him. "I know you have a meeting soon, and I do this often enough and have never had any trouble. You seem to forget that I grew up here."

"There is no way around it, Miss St. Angelo. If you do not take a carriage, then I will escort you. What if something happens to you and Miss Beaumont discovers I was here and allowed you to leave unattended?" He offered Aria his arm again and grinned. "It is futile to argue. I'm a lawyer, you know, and I will win."

Aria's heart stopped at the sight of his smile. *This is getting quite out of control. If someone saw us walking arm in arm in the city and word got back to Mr. Beaumont, I could very easily lose my position.* But again, not wishing to seem rude, she slowly nodded and accepted his arm. *I suppose I could always just tell Mr. Beaumont the truth and pray that he believes me.*

WHILE IT MAY HAVE BEEN a short stroll from the station to the Commercial Hotel where he was staying, the walk to her family's apartment across from Jackson Square was nearly a half hour's walk away, and Byron was once again thankful he accompanied Aria to keep her from harm's way. Even though she claimed it was safe, New Orleans was no place for a pretty woman to walk about unescorted. He tried to remember Mildred's smile and comely face, yet he kept losing her features in Aria's smile that illuminated her dark eyes as well as her lovely face.

Cutting through the square and around the Andrew Jackson equestrian statue, Aria paused at St. Ann Street in front of a four-story red-brick building with french doors lining the first floor and wrought-iron lace balconies wrapping the second and third floors. Judging from the exterior, it had once been a grand apartment building but had fallen into disrepair.

"Well, we have arrived." Her smile looked forced as she added, "I would ask you up to offer you a refreshment, but I know you have to return to the hotel to freshen up before you meet with your client."

Catching the hint that she did not wish for him to continue with her, he bowed and was about to offer his goodbye when two little girls squealed as they barreled into Aria and threw their gangly arms around her waist.

"Aria! You're home!" they shouted.

He watched as Aria's enthusiasm filled her countenance. No longer was she the proper lady's companion. She was a sister who missed her family. Kissing each of them atop their dark brown hair, she exclaimed how they were growing prettier by the day.

When they turned their curious gazes to him, Aria straightened, and with a hand on each of their shoulders, she said, "Mr. Roderick, allow me to introduce you to my sisters Gemma and Teodora."

Byron grinned at the miniature Arias and bowed, sending the girls into a fit of giggles to which Aria rolled her eyes and rubbed her brows with her thumb and forefinger. "It is an honor to meet you two ladies."

Teodora dipped into a wobbly curtsy while Gemma popped her thumb out of her mouth and asked, "Are you our sister's beau?"

Aria winced and dipped her chin as she chided them. "What a question to ask. Of course not. He is courting the lady I work for, Miss Beaumont. We happened by each other on the train from Baton Rouge."

Byron hid his smile behind his hand, laughing inside at her chagrin, when a soft voice called her name. Turning, he saw two more young ladies crossing the street with baskets loaded with laundry balanced against their hips.

"What are you doing here? Did Mr. Beaumont finally convince Millie to let you go?" the taller of the two teased, giving Aria a quick embrace before they both examined him. "And who is this gentleman? Have you finally brought home a caller?"

"Bianca, please." Aria shushed her and, ignoring her questions, she continued, "Mr. Roderick, please excuse my sisters. This is Miss Bianca and"—she turned and gestured to the shorter sister—"Miss Caterina St. Angelo."

Before he could even tip his hat, Bianca asked him, "Won't you come up and join us for dinner? Mama is making meatballs and spaghetti."

"He is busy, I'm sure," Aria interjected, looking up at him when the upstairs window opened and a heavyset woman leaned out. "Aria, don't keep your guest standing outside. Bring him up!"

Aria returned her wave and turned to him with eyes sparkling with mirth as a giggle escaped her lips. "I'm so glad that practically the whole family is here to greet you. I hope you aren't too overwhelmed."

"*Practically* the whole family? How many more of you are there?" He laughed.

"Well, there's still Palo, my brother, and my papa, and, of course, my aunts and uncles and their children, but they live one apartment down from ours. I know you are busy, so please don't feel like you have to stay."

Not wanting to intrude, he tipped his hat to her. "Please tell your mother that I am honored for her invitation, but business keeps me from having the privilege of dining with you all tonight."

She reached for her reticule. "Thank you for accompanying me. It made the time pass quite quickly."

"And for me as well," he admitted with a smile, surrendering the bag to her. Bowing, he left Aria to the endearing chatter of her sisters, thinking how adored she was by her family. . .and by him. He sighed. *Lord, help me to honor my word to my father, for my heart seems to be leaving my head behind for Miss St. Angelo and her enchanting eyes.*

CHAPTER FIVE

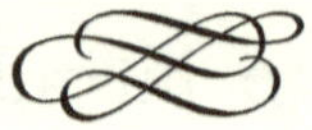

The next morning Byron stopped by the bustling French market on his way back from seeing his clients. He bent down and selected a ripe pear from one of the vendor's crates. Squeezing it to test its tenderness, he decided to purchase a couple and have them for breakfast when he spotted Aria in a powder-blue gown with her sister Bianca near a vegetable vendor, their hands waving wildly as their Italian escalated. While he didn't understand their words, he became worried as their tones grew more and more hostile. Paying the vendor, he tucked the pears into his pocket and wove through the crowded stalls to Aria's side. "Is there a problem here?"

At his voice, Aria jumped and immediately dropped her hands. "Byron!" She stumbled to correct herself. "I mean, Mr. Roderick."

His heart skipped at the sound of his Christian name on her lips. "Is everything all right?" he asked again.

She scowled at the vendor and said something in Italian to him in a reproachful tone, wagging her finger at him before turning to Byron. "It will be," she said with a smile. "Our vendor was trying to charge us *twice* the usual amount. He says figs are in high demand this weekend." With her hands planted on her hips, she looked over her shoulder at the vendor and raised her voice. "Does he think we can be taken advantage of so easily?"

"You aren't the only vendor here," Bianca added to the man, nodding in agreement. "Aria, I'm going across the market to finish Mama's list. Come find me if you see a *reasonable* price for figs, but can you get the pecans?"

Aria nodded and marched over to the next stall.

Byron grinned. Gone was the timid companion. Being home brought a confidence to Aria's shoulders that he quite enjoyed. "So, figs. What are you preparing?"

"Fig cookies for the neighborhood children." She shifted her basket on her arm as she perused the vendors. "It's not much, but we enjoy baking them, and the children have come to look forward to late October because they know that's when Mama's fig cookies will be made."

Byron couldn't help smiling down at her. For a family who obviously struggled to make ends meet, he admired their generosity. He removed the basket from her arm, surprised at its weight. "That sounds delightful. I've never had a fig cookie."

She awarded him a small smile of her own and a nod of thanks. "Grazie. Maybe I can set a few aside for you. We are baking them this afternoon." She paused at a cart and popped a pecan sample into her mouth, nodding with approval. "I'll take two pounds of pecans," she said, counting out the amount as the vendor weighed the nuts. "So, tell me, what are you doing out so early?" She paid the man and set the sack of pecans in the basket.

He laughed, rubbing his eyes under his spectacles. "Well, it's been a long night."

"Long night? You haven't gone to sleep yet?" She lifted her brow.

"I was helping my clients build their case. Normally, I would have come to New Orleans to meet with a client sooner, but the office had me tied up with other cases. They didn't deem Mr. and Mrs. O'Neal's claim against their landlord worth the office's time, especially since they live so far away. Apparently, none of the law offices here would take their case, so they were forced to seek help in Baton Rouge. I was barely able to slip away." He lifted his hat and ran his fingers through his hair, self-conscious of his unkempt state. "Hence the late night. I was on my way back to the hotel to freshen up before I represent them in court."

"How kind of you," she replied as they

approached Bianca, who was filling her basket with figs.

Byron shuffled, feeling uncomfortable. "Please don't think I told you that for praise. I was only trying to explain my disheveled appearance."

"You don't need to explain anything to me. Miss Beaumont knows you are a good man." Aria gave him a sweet smile. "And from the sound of it, your clients think so too."

Something about the corner of her lips seemed familiar. He shook himself as he joined their small party, walking back toward Jackson Square. *Why would her lips seem familiar?* To distract himself, he retrieved the fruit from his pocket and offered the ladies one of the pears. Bianca politely refused, but Aria accepted it.

"Pears are a weakness of mine." She turned her head to take a discreet bite of her fruit.

As you are a weakness of mine. The thought almost stopped him in his tracks. He was enjoying her company far more than Mildred's. *Maybe I am calling on the wrong lady at the Beaumont residence.* With a bow, he left the sisters at the door at the bottom of the Pontalba apartments and returned to the Commercial Hotel.

ARIA'S SIBLINGS were relentless in their teasing as she chopped up figs for the cookie filling. Just when she felt they were through and she could have a moment's peace, her mama finished sifting five pounds of flour into her large bowl and turned to her.

"So, who is this man whom we've seen for the past two days? Should we be inviting him to dinner?" Her thick brows rose, her meaning clear as she measured out the white sugar.

"As I told you before, he is Miss Beaumont's gentleman." Aria finished with the figs and began working on pitting the dates.

"He may be Miss Beaumont's young man, but only in Miss Beaumont's mind. He likes you, daughter. Why else would he escort you 'safely' home twice in two days?"

Mama laughed, shaking her head. "In my day, a young man walking a girl home was a sign of courtship."

"It's not like that," Aria retorted, thumping her knife against the chopping block and sweeping the finely chopped figs, dates, pecans, and raisins into the wooden bowl of spices, sugar, and water before stirring it into a fine paste.

"Mmm-hmm." Her mother humored her as she cracked open the eggs with one hand and kept the other splayed on her lower back, clearly not believing her.

Aria opened her mouth to protest, but the sound of someone pounding on the door intruded. She met her mother's worried gaze and, wiping her hands on her apron, followed her down the stairs. Family and friends would never pound. Peering around Mama's shoulder, Aria stifled a gasp at the sight of a police officer. Seeing a lawman at the Pontalba buildings was never a good sign.

The policeman scowled. "Is Palo St. Angelo here?"

"Why?" Anxiety clouded Mama's voice. "Is something wrong?"

"We received a complaint from one of the merchants that shortly after Palo and his friends left the man's shop, a gold watch was missing from the case where Palo had been lingering."

Mama blanched and reached back for Aria's hand. "Are you accusing my son of theft?"

The officer raised his brow as if it was obvious. "The merchant had a witness."

"That is ridiculous," Aria interjected. "Palo would never rob anyone." *But those boys he keeps company with might. . . .* She pressed her lips into a grim line.

"My son is a good boy. He wants to go to the university and wouldn't dream of—"

"I am only doing my job. I was told to bring in Palo St. Angelo, and I plan to follow through with my orders. Now, will you fetch him, or do I need to come inside and drag him out myself?"

"He's not here." Mama's voice shook.

The officer frowned. "You're only

making this more difficult on yourself, ma'am."

"She's telling the truth. He's down the street at a friend's house." Aria rested a hand on her mother's shoulder, lending her strength. "I'll take you to him." She turned to her mother and whispered, "The officer is only doing his job. There has been some terrible mistake, but it will come out all right. Don't worry, Mama."

"You know that it won't turn out right. It never does for our sort. This will ruin Palo's chances for acceptance at the university, and you've been saving for so long." Mama whimpered into her hands, sinking down on the doorstep. She lifted her apron and hid under the checkered cloth, as if seeking a moment's privacy to gather herself.

Aria knew, as did all the St. Angelo children, not to disturb her when the apron was lifted. She motioned for the officer to walk ahead of her down the sidewalk. "He is right around the corner, sir."

CHAPTER SIX

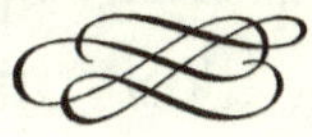

Dressed in her ivory traveling gown, Aria stood in front of the daunting wooden gates with windows of iron bars. She'd promised Mama to take a tin of fig cookies to the jail before boarding her train to Baton Rouge. Straightening her shoulders, she reminded herself of her plan, swallowed, pulled the bell cord, and waited. She could hardly believe that her little brother could be accused of theft much less be held in New Orleans Parish Prison. She would have to be strong for Palo even if she felt like wallowing in despair.

The gates creaked open as if the jail did not receive many visitors or release many prisoners. She shivered, clutching her tin and the Doyle novel with both hands and prayed, *Lord, help him be pardoned quickly.*

The guard waved her inside and quickly closed the gate behind her, barring it from the inside with a large plank. "What's a comely little thing like you doing in a place like this?" His eyes roved over her, causing a blush to creep up her neck.

She lifted her head and, as if daring him to keep his vulgar gaze upon her a moment longer, narrowed her eyes and answered in what she hoped was a clear, strong voice. "I've come to visit my brother, Palo St. Angelo."

"Brought him something, did you?" He nodded to the pretty blue tin with flowers curving around the container. "Let's see it."

Hesitant, she handed him the tin, his calloused, dirty fingers brushing against her kid gloves and leaving smudges as she jerked her hands away from his touch. He popped open the tin Mama had so lovingly prepared. Aria knew it had been a sacrifice for Mama to come up with the extra ingredients to send Palo two dozen cookies to lift his spirits, but the guard seemed uninterested in the care that went into making the treat as he dug his filthy hand into the tin, breaking the crescent-shaped cookies and raking them between his fingers until they became like gooey bread crumbs.

Aria gasped. "Wh–what are you doing?" she sputtered.

Not even bothering to replace the lid, he took the one cookie left unharmed before shoving the tin back into her hands, spilling a few crumbs onto her immaculate gown. "I had to check it for a file or a knife. Don't really trust you Italians since one of your kind murdered Chief Hennessy two years ago."

A knife or a file? Was he jesting? They're just cookies, she wanted to scream. *And we don't particularly trust the people of New Orleans because of what happened afterward either.* She thought of the mob lynching that resulted in so many Italian men's deaths, but she knew to speak of such things wouldn't do any good. "You could have just cut them open instead of destroying two dozen cookies."

The guard's brows rose at her tart reply. "A cookie will taste the same if it looks like a crescent moon or mash." His yellow teeth flashed as he popped the cookie into his mouth and smacked his lips. "Now," he said, sucking his fingers one by one, "if you want to see your brother, I suggest you keep it civil."

Aria clamped her lips shut, wishing she wasn't at this man's mercy, but she swallowed her pride for her brother's sake and dipped her head.

Taking her bowed head as a sign of submission, he grinned and motioned for her to follow him. In the common room, he instructed her to take a seat at one of the tables while he fetched Palo. Perched on the edge of a grimy chair, Aria watched as an enormous cockroach crawled across the ceiling and dropped dangerously close to her. She stifled a scream as she lifted her skirts to keep the disgusting creature from scuttling up her clothes and shivered as it disappeared into a hole in the wall.

The dank, dark room reeked of hopelessness. Through her lashes, she discreetly observed two other couples with their heads bent together, visiting at the small tables dotting the room. Judging from the simple gold bands on the women's fingers and the men's soft, sorrowful gazes, she supposed they were married. *How awful to be separated from the one you love.*

Unwillingly, her thoughts drifted to Byron and his kindness in walking her home. She could only pray that he would answer her petition for help. It would be difficult to get a letter to him with Mr. Beaumont's watchful eye on the post. She would have to wait for a moment when Mildred left the room to ask him to represent Palo. Remembering how compassionate his voice became when he spoke of his pro bono work, she felt confident that he would come to her aid.

The moment Palo appeared in the doorway, all else faded away except the stricken, wide-eyed gaze on her brother's face. She longed to run to him, but with the guard standing by and scowling at her every move, she simply rose from her seat and waited as he shuffled toward her, encumbered by the heavy chains binding his ankles. Tears closed her throat at the sight of his filthy face and torn shirt pocket. *They are treating him like an animal. He is only fifteen, and he hasn't even been found guilty yet. Oh, why didn't I encourage him sooner to give up those rowdy boys? He wouldn't be here if I did. I knew they would get him into trouble.*

Instead of giving into her grief over his loss of innocence, she plastered on a brave smile. "Palo," she whispered, her voice cracking. *No, I must do better.* She embraced him and gave him a peck on the cheek and for once, he did not shy away from her affections. "How are you doing?"

He shrugged, the chains on his ankles clanking as he took the seat opposite her at the table. "I don't think there's much hope for me. There are boys here that have been awaiting trial for six months." He looked up at her, his eyes brimming. "Most of them are pretty sick, and I doubt they will make it to see their day in court."

"But you didn't do anything wrong. Surely that counts for something?" She reached across the table and took his hand in hers.

"The merchant at Brooks and Brooks doesn't care who gets locked up as long as someone does, and we don't have money for a lawyer, unless you use the money you set aside for my college fund," he mumbled. His tone exuded misery as his Adam's apple bobbed.

"It won't come to that. That's partly why I came today, to bring you cookies and some reassurance," she said, lifting the tin. "I know someone who is a lawyer, and I will be seeing him in a couple of days, if not sooner. I'm sure he will be sympathetic to your situation and will see to it that your court date is moved up."

"That's an awful good connection for a lady's companion," he replied, a teasing lilt reappearing in his voice at the prospect of being represented. "It was that fellow who escorted you home yesterday, wasn't it?" He grinned at Aria's blush but didn't press the matter further and nodded toward the tin. "I'll take those cookies now."

She handed him the tin, but before she

could explain its state, he popped it open. At the sight of the crumbled mess, his jaw tightened. He knew the sacrifice it cost to make so many cookies for one person. "No respect," he said through gritted teeth.

"It will still taste the same." She dimly echoed the guard's cruel words. "It will taste of love." She reached out and stroked his cheek, his patchy stubble pricking her fingers. "I wish I could stay longer, little brother, but I have to catch my train." She pressed the book into his hands. "Maybe this will help pass the time. I hope you will enjoy it as much as I did."

A small smile played at the corner of his lips. "Sherlock Holmes? That's quite the switch for you. Thanks. I'll be waiting for your lawyer beau to come for a visit."

Aria blushed again. "His name is Byron Roderick and he is Miss Beaumont's suitor." Despite her gentle chide, she couldn't help but smile at his ability to tease even when in prison.

"Will this Mr. Roderick be able to clear my record? I doubt Louisiana State University will accept a convict."

She squeezed his arm. "Your dream won't die in here. I won't let it."

The guard approached their table with his arms crossed. "Time's up."

The hope in Palo's eyes faded. Aria grabbed him in a fierce hug and bid him farewell. "*Ciao,* Palo. Remember the verse in Joshua. 'Have not I commanded thee? Be strong and of a good courage; be not afraid, neither be thou dismayed: for the Lord thy God is with thee whithersoever thou goest.' The Lord will not abandon you in here, and neither will I."

Palo nodded as the guard grabbed him by the arm and pulled him away. "Hurry," he called over his shoulder.

With the gates closing behind her, Aria strode across the street toward the train station, determined to make her little brother safe once again.

"I HOPE YOUR JOURNEY WAS FRUITFUL?" Father asked as he sank into his favorite leather wingback chair by the fireplace.

Byron removed his coat and stretched his hands toward the fire to take away the chill from his ride over from the station. "I was able to save my clients' lifework and managed to get their rent reduced for a year as recompense for the landlord's actions."

"That's not what I meant and you know it." Father struck a match and lit his cigar. "You were supposed to meet with my friend to discuss that high-profile case. If you take his case and win, your career will be set for life."

Byron sighed. *Are we really going to have this discussion again?* He took the chair opposite his father. "I did meet with him, and while I appreciate the business, I've told you before, Father, that I don't care about having *all* high-profile cases, especially when I don't believe the client is innocent."

"But you should care. I can't be responsible for your finances forever and besides, you need to have experience that will actually *impress* influential voters. A pro bono case here and there is fine, but not every other case can be charity work. I've been grooming you for my seat all these years and it's about time that you show some gratitude and use that law degree I paid for and actually take some prestigious cases that will *pay*."

"I am very grateful to have had your support in school, but since I graduated nearly five years ago, I've offered many times to completely cover my costs so that I may pursue my preferred line of work, but you continually line my pockets."

"That's because we have an image to uphold, son." With his cigar between two fingers, Byron's father rubbed his forehead. "I am thankful you are at least doing something right for your future by courting Miss Beaumont, but promise me that you will stop this nonsense of taking on so many pro bono cases and take some real clients."

They are real clients, Byron wanted to retort, but he swallowed and tried to remain respectful. "I wish I could promise you, sir, but my passions lie with the people. And I assure you, I do not work for free on a majority of the cases."

"A chicken or a basket of baked goods is not what I consider payment. Besides, I keep trying to tell you that you don't have to surrender your passions for the people if you take the state senate seat." He leaned forward, his elbows resting on his thighs. "You will have more power to help those people from that seat than down in the ditches with the rabble."

Byron nodded. "I understand you, sir, and while I agree that the state senate could offer a better foothold to help the poor, I feel that my calling is to help the people by serving them in the ditches, as you put it."

Mr. Roderick grunted and waved him off. "There you go with that 'calling' nonsense. Ever since you started going to that church, you've been impossible. If only your younger brother were finished with his schooling, I'm sure he wouldn't be as ungrateful as his elder brother."

"I know Tom is passionate about politics. If you could wait a little while longer, you will have another Roderick ready to follow in your footsteps, and I will be free to run my practice."

"I don't have any more time! You know

as well as I that the time to begin campaigning is now."

Byron gritted his teeth. Their conversation always seemed to go in circles, never ending. He tried to be respectful to his father, but it was getting harder as time went on and the day for announcing a new candidate approached. "I don't know how to say this, Father, but I don't want to be a state senator."

"Do you think I don't know that?" His father puffed on his cigar, scowling into the embers. "For years, I've dreamt of a dynasty, a legacy of Roderick men in the political world. Your grandfather clawed this family up society's ladder, yet you seem determined to throw our name in the gutter. You keep this up and Mr. Beaumont's daughter won't have you, and then where will I be? Completely abandoned by my own son."

Byron bowed his head, the weight of his father's expectations and disappointment pressing on him. "I'm sorry you feel that way, sir. I would never intentionally harm our family's name. I think that working in the French Quarter, though not as well paid, is just as honorable as a job at the capitol."

Without a word, his father flicked his cigar into the fire, shoved back his chair, and stomped out.

Byron sighed and leaned back in his chair and stared into the flames. Maybe his father was right. Perhaps he should relinquish his dream and pour his efforts into marrying well and winning the seat. He could still make a difference. . .only not in the way he had hoped, or with whom he hoped.

CHAPTER SEVEN

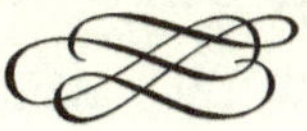

It was too glamorous. Ordinarily, Aria looked forward to attending a musicale for weeks, but with Palo in prison, all she could see was the opulence. How could she pretend to enjoy the quartet, the singing, and the decadent refreshments when all she could think of was Palo, shivering in a damp cell? The letter in her handbag, explaining his situation, weighed on her, but with Mr. Beaumont near, she would have to wait for the right moment to slip it into Byron's hand.

She longed for the songs to transport her to a happier time, but try as she might, every note reminded her that she was out of her class. This group knew nothing of the hardships of her people. The only reason she was here was because of Millie and even then, Mr. Beaumont had barely approved of hiring her. He had only relented when he'd discovered her very distant ties to the Italian aristocracy. While she looked the part of a fine lady, under the refashioned pink ruffles of Millie's discarded gowns, she was still that little girl from St. Ann Street, living in a run-down apartment hand to mouth after her father lost his job. She was the first and the last of her family to attend the fine school where she had met Millie. If Mr. Beaumont ever saw her family's home, she was certain she would be released at once. She glanced out of the corner of her eye at Byron. He had seen where she was from, and yet she knew that he would not hesitate in coming to her aid.

"Aria," Millie whispered to her behind her fan, "I'm not feeling well. I'm supposed to sing in a moment, but I feel as if there is a frog lodged in my throat." She wrapped her gloved fingers around her ivory neck. "I can't possibly go on in my state."

Aria followed Millie's gaze to where Joel Branson stood in the corner of the room without the infamous Fiona on his arm. "Are you sure it isn't just nerves? You've practiced over and over for two weeks. And you know your father would be quite upset if you deferred, especially since Governor Foster's wife is hosting the event."

"I know, but I'm sure I will croak if I go up there now." Mildred's eyes widened. "I've never sung in front of Jo—I mean, anyone before." She flapped her fan to cool her burning cheeks. "I wish you could sing for me. If only you could pretend to be me once more."

"The only way we could pull that off is if I stood behind the curtain and sang while you mouthed the words." Aria giggled into her hand at the ludicrous notion.

"That's it!" Millie gripped both of Aria's hands in her own, giving them a little shake.

"What's it?" Aria blinked, not following her friend.

"You'll sing for me from behind the curtain." Millie squealed, grabbing Aria's wrist and pulling her toward the makeshift stage that resembled a miniature of the one in the opera house.

Aria jerked them to a halt. "You can't be serious. I was completely jesting, Millie. We would be caught after two lines!"

"We could completely pull it off. You know the words. You've heard me practice it about five thousand times," she said, pushing Aria behind the curtain. "Now, you wait here and when you hear them announce me, be ready and listen for the opening notes."

Before Aria could protest further, Millie disappeared. Aria rubbed her forehead. "How on earth do I get roped into these things?" she muttered to herself as the current soloist finished her ballad.

Aria peered through a sliver in the curtain and caught sight of Mr. Beaumont in the front row with a vacant seat to his right, giving Millie an encouraging smile as she took the stage. The pianist began the introduction and taking a deep breath, Aria prayed that Millie knew what she was doing and wouldn't get her fired for this ridiculous scheme.

As she sang, the lyrics of "The Song That Reached My Heart" enveloped her, and she nearly lost herself in their beauty, her eyes finding Byron as he took his seat next to Mr. Beaumont. Her heart burned as she watched his gaze transform as her voice filled the room and she caught the first hint of love cross his face. He was falling for Mildred's voice. . .*her* voice. She returned her gaze to Millie's lips, determined not to fail. At the more difficult parts, Millie flicked her fan in front of her face, conveniently hiding her lips.

When the song concluded, the room erupted in applause and Aria couldn't help but smile at Millie's performance as she curtsied and bowed her head to the audience while they tossed flowers at her feet. Mrs. Foster walked onto the stage to personally congratulate her and announce intermission.

Aria quietly slipped away from the curtain, and once she was as far away from the stage as possible, she made certain that she was seen to allay any suspicion as Byron rose and escorted a beaming Millie from the stage. Aria caught Millie glancing out of the corner of her eye toward Mr. Branson in the corner, a satisfied smirk playing on her lips as if she could sense his jealousy at seeing Byron dote upon her.

Good. She deserves his attention, Aria thought, and followed behind as Byron escorted Millie to the refreshment table for a glass of punch, praising her performance all the while.

"You are fortunate that came off well," Mr. Beaumont murmured into his glass of punch, appearing at her elbow.

Aria paled. *Of course, he would know.*

"Calm yourself, Miss St. Angelo. No one else caught on to your little ruse or else Mildred wouldn't have been so well received. But, as it seems Mr. Roderick is quite smitten with her so-called voice, I suggest that you give up singing for the remainder of your time under my roof. We cannot risk him discovering the truth prior their marriage," he added before stepping away to speak with Governor and Mrs. Foster.

Aria took a deep breath and joined Byron and Millie, overhearing him say, "When you mentioned you could sing, I had no idea that you were such a songbird, Miss Beaumont."

Millie flicked open her fan, dipping her head in false modesty at his praise. "It was nothing. I hardly practiced at all."

Aria refrained from rolling her eyes as she stood behind Millie with her hands folded in front of her skirt, waiting for her chance to speak with Byron alone.

Millie's fan fluttered fiercely. "Would you mind fetching us some pastries, Mr. Roderick? I'm feeling a bit famished from all the excitement."

"Of course." He bowed, excusing himself, but not before his eyes met Aria's, sending a shiver down her spine.

In his gaze, everything around her faded as it had that first night they met.

Millie drew Aria to her side, breaking her trance, and nodded toward the other side of the room. Aria followed her gaze to see Joel grinning at Millie. *Oh no.* "Would you like me to ask him to leave you be?" Aria asked, knowing how sensitive she was about seeing Joel Branson after their separation.

"No," she said, downing the last of her punch. "I'm determined to speak with him."

"You're what? Are you sure that's a good idea, Millie?" She looked over her shoulder to Byron. "People know of your past with him, and if you are seen with Mr. Branson, there will be talk."

Millie shoved her glass into Aria's hands. "Of course it's a good idea. I heard that his latest triumph, *Fiona*,"—she dragged out the name as if it disgusted her—"is in the powder room. With a face like hers, she'll be in there awhile, so what better time is there to speak with him alone without Father or that girl watching our every move?"

"But, you are here with—"

"Distract Byron. I'll only be gone for ten minutes." Millie waltzed across the room and tapped Mr. Branson's arm with her fan, whispering something up to him. Aria watched as his eyes grew wide and he nodded, escorting Millie out to the veranda for a private tête-à-tête.

Aria shook her head and finished her punch, setting the empty glass aside when she felt a hand grasp her elbow. She turned to find Byron returning with napkins and a small dessert plate holding three cannolis dipped in dark chocolate, starting her mouth to watering.

"Where is Miss Beaumont? I brought the refreshments she requested," he said, lifting his plate in offering.

"She had to speak with someone." She hoped the vague answer would suffice, knowing Millie would end her employment if she revealed Millie's secret tryst.

He nodded but didn't appear vexed as he handed her a napkin for her pastry. "Then let's enjoy these before the music begins."

Not caring that a cannoli was a tad too messy for public consumption, she prayed for the courage to ask for his help and bit into the treat.

BYRON COULDN'T BELIEVE it when he had discovered Aria behind the curtain. He had been searching for a program when he overheard Millie's song announced and Aria's voice filled the air. He could have listened and observed her sing for hours, but knowing Mr. Beaumont was waiting, he hurried to his seat to watch Millie's performance of a lifetime, thinking it was little wonder why he didn't have a connection with Millie. She had never been the one behind the mask.

To test his theory, he retrieved the one thing he knew would solidify the masked woman's identity and watched as Aria ate the cannoli. No other lady besides the one woman he met that first night weeks ago would chomp into a pastry with such fervor.

Aria handed the soiled napkin to a passing waiter and kept speaking, but all he could think of was, why would she lie to him? He knew that Miss Beaumont's father only wanted him for his daughter because of his connections, so perhaps he was the one behind Aria's masquerade. While he felt that he should be angry learning the truth, he only felt a sense of relief, for it explained why he didn't feel drawn to Mildred and why he was so attracted to Aria. Miss Beaumont's companion was the masked songbird.

With this revelation, he knew that trouble would follow. Because of Mildred's budding friendship with the governor's wife, he had told his father he was seeing a woman who would help his father's political career, but now, he discovered he was in love with Mildred's companion. He drew up abruptly at the thought. *Am I in love with her?* He contemplated all the times his thoughts drifted to Beaumont Manor not because of Mildred, but because of Aria and her smiling eyes. His father would not be happy, but now that Byron had found her, he would not let her go.

"Mr. Roderick?" Aria looked up to him, confusion in her gaze. "Are you quite well?"

He blinked. "I'm sorry, did you ask me a question? I'm afraid I was deep in thought."

"Yes, but, um, I can ask you again tomorrow if you, um. . ." Aria bit her lip and looked down at her hands before smoothing the front of her pink skirt and glancing at nearby guests.

The concerned lines above her brow stirred him. "Pardon my distraction. What is it that you needed to ask?"

She dipped her head and picked at the lace trim on her fan. "I'm sorry to bother you during the musicale, but I didn't know when I might be able to catch you alone again, and the delicate matter I wish to discuss cannot wait."

The tremble in her voice alarmed him. He gently took her elbow and guided her to the corner of the room near a floor-length window. "Please, continue."

"I had hoped to catch you outside of the courthouse last week, but you hailed a carriage so quickly I wasn't able to catch your attention." A pretty blush crept over her cheeks. "And by the time I reached the hotel, you had already left for dinner. The hotel desk clerk wasn't willing to disclose at which restaurant you were dining, but when I told them you were courting my employer, they told me to leave a note." She babbled all in a rush, her voice wavering and eyes on the brink of overflowing with suppressed tears.

"I didn't receive any note."

"That's because I have it here." She dug into her reticule and handed him a folded and sealed note. "It was too sensitive to leave with just anyone."

He thought of the dark alleyways surrounding her home in the French Quarter, and his blood ran cold. "Did something happen to you while you were home?" He pocketed the note and motioned for her to take one of the chairs lining the wall, aching to help her in any way he could.

"No, it's my brother." She twisted a handkerchief between her hands and glanced over her shoulder. "You can read about it later. I don't want to bother you with it now."

"It's no bother. Please, let's sit so you can tell me what's wrong. You look positively ill." He ran his hands through his hair at the sight of her tears.

Aria sank into the seat, her fingers curled around her handkerchief as if she were petrified of it being ripped away from her. "I'm afraid my employer would not look kindly on what I'm about to disclose, so I beg for your discretion."

"Of course." He set his plate on the vacant seat next to him.

She looked up at him, her eyes wide and bottom lip trembling. "I can't paint this into a pretty picture. All I can say is that there's been a horrible misunderstanding." She lowered her head. "My brother, Palo, was accused of theft," she whispered.

No wonder she is so distressed. He knew how much she adored her brother. Leaning back in his chair, he pressed his fingers together into a steeple and lifted them to his lips, tapping contemplatively. "Is he guilty?"

Indignation filled her features at his audacious question. "No."

She half rose as if to leave, but he placed his hand on hers, staying her. "Please, it's my job to ask." She returned to her seat, her eyes dropping to his hand holding her own. He quickly released her and settled back, quite aware of the impropriety of touching in public, much less at an event to which he had escorted another woman. The clink of crystal glasses and laughter shook him out of his reverie and, clearing his throat, he leaned toward her. "Tell me everything you know."

CHAPTER EIGHT

Aria barely finished her tale when Fanny Branson appeared in front of them with her hands on her hips.

"There you are!" She lifted one brow at the sight of the two of them seated together. "I have been looking for Miss Beaumont for nearly a quarter of an hour. Do you know where your charge is, Miss St. Angelo?"

Reluctantly, she rose and Byron followed suit. "I believe she was speaking with someone on the veranda," Aria admitted.

"Well, you shouldn't keep Mr. Roderick a moment longer, as intermission is nearly over and he should fetch her." Fanny pursed her lips at him. "After all, you did escort her, did you not?"

"Of course." A hint of annoyance clouded Byron's voice.

Aria's heart thudded with dread, as he hadn't given her an answer yet. She longed to have more time with him to discuss Palo's fate, but she knew she had to maintain a calm façade in front of Miss Branson or risk being discovered and losing her position. *So many secrets. First my deception with Byron at the masquerade and now I have to keep this from Mr. Beaumont.*

"I shall see to your request, Miss St. Angelo." He gave her a short bow before slipping away to find Millie.

"Do you not care about Miss Beaumont's reputation?" Fanny hissed.

Aria's stomach dropped. *Surely, she didn't overhear us?* "Pardon?"

"How could you allow her to venture out onto the veranda alone? She is obviously speaking with my brother, who is as good as engaged. Do your duty and go to her this instant or I shall inform Mr. Beaumont of your tête-à-tête with Mr. Roderick. Regardless, I'll be warning Miss Beaumont."

Aria lifted her head. "We spoke of nothing flirtatious, I assure you."

"Miss Beaumont is my friend, and I won't sit idly by and allow you to throw yourself at her beau. You are a distraction, and she needs to be put on her guard."

As long as it's not Mr. Beaumont, tell the world, Aria wanted to retort. Instead, she answered, "As you wish. Please excuse me." She hurried toward the french doors when she spotted Millie returning from the veranda with flushed cheeks.

Instead of heading toward Byron, who had been intercepted by Mr. Beaumont, Millie twisted around until her eyes found Aria's. With brisk steps, she crossed the floor and snagged Aria by the elbow, whispering, "We need to go. *Now.*"

Confused, Aria scrunched her eyebrows. "Now? Is something wrong? Did you tear your dress?" She glanced at Millie's emerald gown and only found a tiny smear on her glove. "Did your father wish for us to leave early?"

"It's nothing like that and no, Father doesn't know. Trust me and come. We are done here for the night." Millie pulled her toward the front room.

"But what about Byron? You can't leave your escort, especially at the governor's mansion," Aria protested.

"Watch me."

"Mildred!" Aria yanked her arm away, halting them both. She gritted her teeth, and with a smile meant to keep others from suspecting an argument, she added softly, "Mr. Roderick has been nothing but kind to both of us, and I can't allow you to do that. You can at least spare two minutes while I tell him that we are leaving and you bid Mrs. Foster a proper farewell. Your father will have my hide if you do not."

Millie sighed and rolled her eyes. "Fine, but please do hurry. We don't have much time. I'll explain at home."

Aria slipped away and, scanning the room, spied Byron speaking with an elderly gentleman. Not wanting to interrupt, but not daring to be caught in a drawn-out conversation, she waved him to her, praying he would come before the two minutes were up. "I'm sorry," she whispered when he reached her, "but Millie and I must leave."

"Is she unwell?"

"I'm not exactly sure what is going on, but it seems that she wishes for a bit of privacy, so we will take Mr. Beaumont's carriage and have it sent back for him." Aria glanced over her shoulder to ensure that Millie was distracted. "Will I see you soon about. . . ?"

He gently touched his lips to her glove, sending a jolt to her spine. "Yes, I'd like to discuss how to proceed with your brother's case in a more private setting. Perhaps we could meet at the coffeehouse tomorrow morning, say, nine o'clock?"

Aria blushed and quickly withdrew her hand, hoping he did not feel her trembling. Though she knew she shouldn't risk being seen with him in public, she had to for Palo. And if she were honest with herself, she secretly ached to spend more time alone with him even if society considered him as good as promised to Millie. "Perfect." She dipped into a curtsy and rushed away for fear Millie would ask what was taking so long.

"Finally," Millie grunted, pushing Aria through the doors and into a waiting carriage. "Hurry now, before Father tries to follow."

"What is with all this cloak-and-dagger nonsense?" Aria asked as she settled her skirts around her on the seat. "Why do we have to leave so suddenly?"

Millie waved her off, her eyes alight with excitement and her cheeks flushed as she peeled off her gloves and lowered the window. "Is it hot in here to you?"

"It's November," Aria said, her voice flat. Something wasn't right. *Did Mr. Branson ask for her hand in marriage? And is she rushing home to avoid her father stopping her from doing something foolish?* Aria wanted to inquire further, but she knew Millie wouldn't reveal even a smidgeon of her plan until it was too late to give her any form of advice. So Aria remained silent, staring out the window and trying unsuccessfully to not think of a certain pair of hazel eyes.

Lord, I know I cannot have him, but now

that he has agreed to help Palo, I fear my heart is lost to him forever. Unbidden, tears streaked down her cheeks, but before Millie could notice, she brushed away any trace as the carriage halted in front of Beaumont Manor.

When they were about halfway up the main stairs, Mr. Beaumont hailed them from the front door.

"Girls! Get down here," he barked, tearing off his top hat and handing it and a riding crop to the butler.

Millie's cheeks paled. "How did he find out? And how did he catch up with us?" she whispered more to herself than to her companion as they followed him into the cold parlor.

Spying Mr. Beaumont's red face under his furrowed brows, Aria cringed. *He must have followed us with alarming speed to match his temper, which does not bode well for you, Millie.* She slipped into the room behind Millie with her head bowed slightly and hands folded, waiting for his wrath to descend upon Millie for whatever crime she had been scheming.

"When were you going to tell me about your brother?" Mr. Beaumont's angry gaze burned into Aria, startling her. "When the scandal was laid at our doorstep? It's bad enough to have you here with your. . .background, but I had to find out at the *governor's* musicale from my colleague that his daughter overheard you mention your brother's conviction."

Her heart hammered in her chest. *Fanny.* She gripped the back of the settee to steady herself.

Mildred whipped around, her mouth ajar. "What is he talking about?"

Ignoring his daughter, Mr. Beaumont continued. "And when I went to find you, Mr. Roderick informed me that you had both left in *my* carriage, forcing me to borrow a steed." He threw his arms up. "Honestly, if you wished to keep this from me, did you not think that *someone* would overhear you if you confessed his transgressions in a crowded room?"

Aria managed to meet his gaze even as her knees quaked beneath her skirts. "I'm sorry, sir. I thought discretion was best suited for this situation, as my brother is innocent. He merely needs to have his name cleared."

"And how could you afford for him to be found innocent? A good lawyer is the only thing that stands between him and prison. I cannot have my daughter's companion related to a convict," he shouted, jabbing his finger at Aria.

Millie gasped, pressing a handkerchief to her eyes. "Father, you can't. I'm sure—"

"Palo will not be a convict. Mr. Roderick has agreed to represent him," Aria said, desperate for the chance to save her position.

"You approached Byron Roderick? That's whom you were telling?" The vein in his forehead rose. "Impudent girl! How dare you address my daughter's suitor under the governor's roof! If Foster catches wind of this, which he will, he will think I have no authority over my employees. What made you think that Roderick would even help you? You've never said more than two sentences to him."

She swallowed back her fear and hastened to explain. "We met quite by chance on the train to New Orleans and—"

"So, you got a taste of the high life at the masquerade ball and now you think you can waltz in and steal a lad from the upper crust because you managed to get him to call on 'you' after the ball." He let out a short laugh. "I would have you remember that he wasn't calling on you. He was calling on *Mildred's* position, *her* wealth and *her* connections."

His words couldn't have stung more if he had slapped her. "I wasn't trying to usurp Millie's beau." *How could I? I have nothing to offer him.*

"I won't stand for it." He huffed. "I was prepared to let you go with a reference even after the scandal you've brought into our house, but now to discover that you were attempting to steal my Mildred's love—"

"He's not my love. She's welcome to him," Millie interjected, threading her arm around Aria's waist, offering her strength. "I was going to call it off after tonight anyway."

Her father held up a hand, halting her once again. "You don't have to defend her, my dear girl. Miss St. Angelo, you have put my daughter's future in jeopardy. She is nothing without her reputation. You are to leave here at once."

Aria dipped her head. "I understand, sir. I will leave first thing in the morning."

"No." He scowled, his brows nearly meeting. "I mean tonight."

"But Father, it's far too dark for a proper lady to leave a house unescorted." Millie's wide-eyed gaze darted to Aria.

"Tonight," he roared.

Aria clenched her fists. *After all I've done for him, he would throw me out on the street like a beggar.* "Mr. Beaumont, you can't possibly expect me to take public transportation at this time of night. It would be quite dangerous to take the last train out to New Orleans unaccompanied."

"I don't care. Your disregard of the boundaries set for a lady's companion makes you too dangerous to keep under my roof. Your very presence could ruin Mildred's reputation and her chances for a good match forever. Go pack at once." He stood by the door, motioning her to make her way through the threshold. "You are fortunate that I am being kind enough to even allow you time for packing."

Aria stiffened and, pressing her lips into a thin line, replied, "I will need my wages."

"Insolent—" he began.

Millie stepped in front of Aria. "Father, we owe her that much," she reprimanded him softly. "She cannot safely return home without her wages."

He dug into his pocket and, counting out an amount, tossed the bills onto the floor and brushed by the two girls, shouting, "Take it and get out of my house."

With a heated face, Aria stiffly retrieved the bills, folding them and tucking them into her reticule before Millie gently grasped her arm and led her up the stairs. "What am I to do?" Aria whispered to her friend.

"You will come with me," she answered emphatically, letting them into Aria's small blue room.

"What? Where are you going?"

Millie shut the bedroom door behind them and turned her excited gaze to Aria.

"It's why we left the musicale early. Joel and I are eloping."

"Eloping? Millie, have you taken leave of the senses the good Lord gave you?"

Millie pressed her hand to her chest. "I have just generously offered to save you from a terrible fate. Don't insult me. Joel and I talked it out, and I can tell you about it on the way to meet him," she said, dragging Aria's trunk from the closet.

"I should tell your father." Aria sank onto the bed, too stunned to pack.

"Why? You see how he would do anything to protect our precious reputation. He will not stop until I'm married off like all my sisters." Millie began tossing Aria's clothes into the trunk. "You best hurry. Father won't allow you much more time."

"Except Byron is a good man." *And not to mention, the most handsome one I've ever met.* She stiffly began gathering her things as Millie went through the adjoining door.

"And you know Joel is a good man. He only ceased his courtship because he needs a little more money than what Father was intending to give us," Millie replied a bit too loudly from her room before carrying in an armload of dresses.

No, I don't know. Aria rubbed her temples. "But your father is still offering the same amount. So why would Joel suddenly change his mind?"

Millie grinned, dropping her garments onto Aria's bed. "You see, that's where we figured if we eloped, Father would have to give us more money or else we would say we wed without his blessing. Faced with such a scandal, he wouldn't balk at an extra few thousand."

"Mildred Eloise Beaumont!" Aria gasped, nearly dropping her small framed portrait of her family.

"Brilliant, isn't it? I've seen how Father plays his politician's game." She giggled. "I bet he never thought I'd be brazen enough to try something so daring, but he pushed us into a corner. What did he expect me to do?"

"I don't know, maybe marry Byron Roderick? He is a wonderful man. And what if Mr. Branson decides *not* to go through with the wedding? He will ruin your reputation and any chance you have of a happy marriage." She cringed at echoing Mr. Beaumont's words, but knew that despite his cruelty, he was right. Mildred's reputation must be protected.

"With you there to chaperone, it will be more than proper until our vows are spoken." Eyeing the clock, she flew between the two rooms, stuffing both of their things into Aria's trunks. At Aria's confused look, she explained, "I need to make it look like everything is yours and not mine. Father won't blink at you having an extra trunk, but three would raise brows, so I must stuff everything into two."

Aria felt torn on whether or not to notify Mr. Beaumont, but she knew that once Millie set her mind to something, she wouldn't change it even if she discovered halfway through that she was in over her head. If she didn't elope tonight, Millie would find another way into Joel's arms. At least this way, Aria could watch over her. As her lady's companion, or former companion, she felt duty bound to protect Millie's reputation even if it meant going along with her harebrained scheme.

"Are you sure you want to go through with this? Once you leave with Mr. Branson, there is no returning," she warned.

"Why would I want to return?" Millie snorted, slamming the trunk lid shut.

Because you have a father who loves you and more wealth than I could ever imagine. "Then I will act as your chaperone this one last time and will not leave your side until the vows have been spoken and a ring is on your finger, declaring that you are legally Mrs. Joel Branson."

"Thank you!" Millie squealed and embraced her before giving a little twirl and sighing as she repeated, "Mrs. Joel Branson."

The footmen appeared at the door, and Henry, the shorter of the two, gave Aria a sad smile and announced, "It's time."

Aria tied on her cloak over her fine dress and gave Millie a hug.

"I'll see you soon," Millie whispered into her ear, giving Aria's elbow a squeeze.

With arms crossed and a biting remark,

Mr. Beaumont surveyed Aria's shameful exodus from the manor. Knowing she wouldn't be allowed to say her farewells to the staff, she bid farewell to the two footmen carrying her things and nodded in passing to one of the maids. "Please give Cook and the rest my best wishes," she whispered.

The maid dipped her head but made no response, fear flickering in her eyes as Mr. Beaumont bellowed for Aria to move along.

"If you don't leave this instant, I won't allow you the use of my carriage to the station, young lady," he warned.

Aria squeezed the maid's arm and, with her satchel and reticule in hand, rustled out into the damp night. The footmen harnessed her two trunks stuffed with her and Millie's things onto the back of the carriage while Aria looked over her shoulder one last time at the manor that had been her home for the past five years. She had treasured her time under the Beaumont roof and the benefits that had come with being Millie's companion. With a sigh, she slipped inside the carriage and almost shrieked when she saw a form occupying the corner.

"Shh!" Millie whispered, pressing her gloved hand to Aria's mouth.

"I thought you were meeting me there later! How did you—?" Aria sputtered.

"I told the maids to tell Father I was going to bed early out of protest of your dismissal, so no one will miss me until morning and maybe not even until the afternoon since they think I'll be sulking." She grinned as they started toward the train station. "Maybe your being fired is really a blessing in disguise."

With each bump in the road, Aria silently questioned if going along with Millie's plan was the right thing to do, but Millie chatted so much about her upcoming nuptials that it was difficult to even formulate a sentence, much less an argument, for Millie to abandon her plan.

Reaching the station, Millie practically leaped out of the carriage and into the waiting arms of her intended. "Joel," she said with a sigh, resting her head against his chest.

"My darling, I was worried you wouldn't come," he whispered into her hair.

"Why wouldn't I?" She lifted her gaze to meet his, her love exuding from every feature.

"Well, for one, I thought you wouldn't be able to keep the secret and your companion would talk you out of it." He chortled and traced her chin with a curved finger.

"Believe me, I tried." Aria stepped out of the shadows as Mr. Branson bent to kiss Millie.

Mr. Branson jerked up, his gaze darkening. "What is *she* doing here? Mildred, I thought I told you—"

"Father fired her and was determined to throw her out of the house this very night, so I thought I would bring her along as our chaperone until we're married. You aren't angry with me, are you, my darling?" Millie rubbed her hand up and down his arm as if to warm him to the idea of Aria joining them.

"I could never be vexed with you." To Millie, he gave a smile, but Aria could see beyond Millie's enchanted gaze that Mr. Branson was livid, and his anger made her suspicious.

If his intentions are honorable, why would he hesitate at protecting her reputation? She bit her lip as the porters carried the luggage to the train. *If they don't wed before the morning and are unchaperoned. . .* She shuddered with the realization of what he had intended to pull on her naive charge. *Mr. Branson was going to use the scandal to pressure Mr. Beaumont into a ghastly amount.* She frowned at the back of his jacket as he purchased another first-class ticket. *Scoundrel. Mr. Beaumont was right to push him away from Millie.*

Aria clutched her satchel and reticule and marched up to Millie's side, determined to keep her eye on Mr. Branson. Instead of allowing him to sit beside Millie in the first-class compartment, she planted herself on the plush seat next to her charge. Mr. Branson raised a brow at her, but she returned his stare with a defiant one of her own, daring him to argue with her. She knew what he was up to and she would not allow him to get away with it. She would see to it that Millie's reputation was guarded until the very end.

Aria kept the corner of her eye trained

on the couple and gazed out the window, wondering when she would ever see Byron Roderick again and if he would travel to New Orleans Parish Prison to see her brother even though she wouldn't be at the coffeehouse in the morning. *Dear Lord, have him help my brother despite all that I've done to him and what Millie's running away will do to his pride. Let me not have spoiled the only chance my brother has of being released from prison unscathed.*

Not seeming to sense the tension in the compartment, Millie kept the conversation flowing with bubbling excitement while Mr. Branson kindly nodded and replied whenever he could. While Aria thought his tone suggested that he did love Millie in his own way, his actions and flagrant disregard for her reputation proved his love of money was greater and that he would go to any extreme to see to it he was compensated for marrying Mildred Beaumont.

After a very long ride to New Orleans, they took a hired carriage to the church Mr. Branson had mentioned to Mildred, but as Aria had guessed, it was closed, and no amount of pounding on the parsonage door would wake the pastor.

"What are we going to do?" Millie's voice spiraled out of control along with her composure as the full weight of her circumstances overwhelmed her.

Aria squeezed her elbow. "Don't worry. We will return first thing in the morning and until then, I'll see to it that you are taken care of, so there will be no call for society to declare that you were caught in a compromising position." She turned to Mr. Branson and said with a clipped tone, "I suggest the Commercial Hotel. Let's be off before we are spotted."

Mr. Branson sighed and escorted the women back inside the waiting carriage. In a matter of minutes they were in the hotel lobby, standing at the front desk as Mr. Branson ordered three rooms.

Whenever they traveled in the past, Millie and Aria had separate rooms, but tonight, she would not let her charge out of her sight. Stepping forward, she whispered to Millie, "It will be best for your reputation if I stay with you the entirety of the night."

Overhearing her, Mr. Branson interjected, "I hardly think it is necessary."

Does he think I'm stupid? She scowled. "Do you care for Miss Beaumont so little? Protect your bride-to-be, Mr. Branson, and book two rooms instead of three," she demanded, staying all arguments.

The frazzled front desk clerk returned his gaze to Mr. Branson. "Sir?"

He sighed and flicked his hand, relenting. "We will take just the two rooms."

Aria leaned forward, adding, "And make them on *separate* floors."

Mr. Branson rolled his eyes, nearly growling as he paid the deposit.

It was going to be a long, restless night watching over Millie. *I will not fail Millie, not on my last night as her companion.*

CHAPTER NINE

Byron checked his pocket watch for the tenth time. *Where is she?* His knee bounced as he tapped the worn wooden table with his spoon. He looked through the wavy windowpanes from his seat in the corner of the coffeehouse and sighed. At the throat clearing from the table next to him, he realized the three cups of coffee he'd downed without food was beginning take a toll on him. He set aside his spoon and, instead, let his anxiety out by polishing his spectacles until they shone. It wasn't like Aria to not follow through with a promise. While he had never met with her before on his own, he knew that whenever

Millie set an appointment, Aria was always there, strictly punctual, with her charge in tow.

Now that he knew he had spent that glorious first evening dancing with Aria and not with the politician's daughter, he had decided to break it off with Miss Beaumont. He only needed to confront Aria and find out once and for all why she lied to him even though he had a pretty fair idea Mr. Beaumont was behind the whole situation.

When the waiter came by for an embarrassing third time asking for his order, Byron decided that something must've come up and Aria couldn't get away, so he quickly paid for his cups of coffee and headed for Beaumont Manor with his hat in hand to find his masked lady and help rescue her brother. The thought that Aria had come to him in her need warmed him on the chilly walk as the last of the leaves crunched beneath his boots. With each stride, he grew more and more determined that no matter what Aria confessed, he would see this lad received justice. The only payment he desired was a dimpled smile from Palo's pretty sister.

Letting the knocker fall against the mahogany door, he stepped back and waited until one of the maids answered.

Upon seeing him, her eyes widened and she dropped into a curtsy. "Mr. Roderick! Please, do come in. I'll fetch the master." She showed him into the parlor and in a matter of seconds, Mr. Beaumont came charging inside.

"Roderick." He rubbed his hand over his haggard face and sighed, gesturing for Byron to take a seat. "I have to admit, I am surprised to see you."

"Why would you be surprised to see me, sir? I know it's a bit early, but I usually call for Miss Beaumont on my lunch break." He rested his hat on his knee, as the frazzled maid had forgotten to take it from him.

Mr. Beaumont's shoulders slumped as he rested both hands on the back of the settee opposite Byron. "Well, I suppose word will spread to you soon enough. I awoke this morning to discover that Mildred has run off."

Byron's stomach dropped as he stood. "Miss Beaumont is gone? Did she leave a note?"

"A handful of her things are packed. I half hoped that she ran off with you, but I fear the worst." He tipped his head back, letting out a long breath. "She's gone, and no doubt so is that scoundrel, Joel Branson. If I get my hands on him—"

"What did Miss St. Angelo have to say? Did she know of Miss Beaumont's plans?" Byron gripped the rim of his hat. To pretend to be someone under duress was one thing, but to lie to a man about the whereabouts of his daughter was another. *She wouldn't. Not Aria.*

"I know not. She is gone as well." He dug his hands into his pockets and stared into the fireplace.

"Then Miss Beaumont's reputation is safe." He gave a breathless laugh. "Surely you have comfort in that, sir."

"I cannot say for certain that they left together," Mr. Beaumont replied, reaching for the pitcher of water on the side table and pouring himself a glass.

"Well, why would Miss St. Angelo leave without her charge? Unless maybe she was following her to stop Miss Beaumont?" He thought out loud, raking his hands through his hair at the thought of the two women leaving the protection of the manor.

"I cannot say for certain, because I fired Miss St. Angelo last night due to the shame she has brought upon our family by keeping her brother's plight a secret and further shame for including my daughter's beau in her nonsense. I sent her away the moment we returned from the musicale."

"You sent her away in the dark? You cannot be serious." Byron could not believe it of the man. Miss St. Angelo might be poor, but she was trained as a gentlewoman and besides, the night was not a safe time for any woman of character to be out alone.

"I lent her a carriage to the station." He shrugged, dismissing Byron's concern. "I'm done with her and have nothing further to say in regard to her well-being." His eyes narrowed. "Why do you care?"

Because if I have anything to do with it, the

lady is my future wife. Byron made for the door.

"Where are you going?" Mr. Beaumont called after him, following him out into the hallway.

Byron tugged on his hat, pausing only to find his coat on the coatrack. "I'm going to find Miss St. Angelo. It seems you have Miss Beaumont's well-being in hand, and I must see to Aria's, as no one else in this house will."

" 'Aria,' is it?" His brows rose. "You care for my daughter's companion," he stated.

"Of course. She has become a dear friend during my time calling on your daughter. A time that has now come to close," Byron added. He had intended to quietly end things with Mildred this morning, but if she had run off with another man, then she had saved him the trouble.

"Never fear. I'm sure Mildred's reputation is quite safe if she left with Miss St. Angelo. If she has tainted it in any way in your eyes, I will see to it that you are compensated accordingly." Mr. Beaumont crossed his arms, waiting for Byron to accept his terms.

Byron clenched his fists. "You act as if this is a business deal."

Mr. Beaumont gave a short laugh. "Don't act like it isn't for you as well. Everyone knows you are being groomed to take the office. Your father is benefiting from this union just as much as I am."

Byron scowled. "Consider any agreement terminated. If Miss Beaumont was here this morning, I would have ended my suit anyway. I know she wasn't the lady I met the first night."

His jaw dropped. "I don't believe my ears. You would give up my daughter for that little Italian woman?"

"That 'little Italian woman' is a lady, and yes. Yes, I would."

EXHAUSTED from her whirlwind morning of seeing Millie safely married to Branson, Aria gripped the wooden handle of her umbrella to keep it from flying off in the torrential downpour. She shuffled down the sidewalk toward her home, her spirits feeling as soaked as her skirts. *What am I to do now, Lord? How am I supposed to tell Mama I lost my position? Who will hire me when I don't even have a recommendation? What am I to do?*

Nearly in tears, she let herself inside to find the house abnormally quiet. Taking the stairs to the kitchen on the second floor, she peeked in to find her mother kneading bread on the wooden countertop.

"Mama?" she croaked.

Her mother whirled around with a rolling pin in hand. "Aria, what on earth?" Seeing her daughter's red eyes and wet skirts, she crossed the room and embraced her, paying no mind to the flour covering her apron or her sticky rolling pin. "Why, you are soaked through! I was just about to let this bread rise and make a café au lait. Come sit and I'll make us a cup." She fluttered to the stove as the milk began to boil.

"Where is everyone?" Aria sank into a wooden chair at the table.

"Bianca and Caterina are out delivering laundry, and the littles are at your aunt's house," her mother answered, pouring the hot milk over the fresh coffee before stirring in a generous spoonful of sugar. "But tell me why are you here and not with Miss Beaumont?" Setting the café au laits on the table, she retrieved a hardened loaf of narrow bread and sliced off two pieces.

"I've ruined everything." Aria buried her face in her arms.

"What are you talking about?"

"I was fired from my position. I am so sorry," she said through her sobs.

Mama came around her chair and wrapped her arms around Aria. "Oh, my sweet girl."

Aria wiped her eyes with the back of her hand. "How on earth are we going to make ends meet now that I've lost my income?"

Mama sank into the chair beside Aria and slid the coffee toward her. She handed her a piece of bread. "Now don't you go worrying. The Lord will provide."

"I was providing through my position, but now that's gone. What are we going to do? How is Palo supposed to go to college? How are the little girls going to get new dresses for school? Papa works so hard, and it's still not enough. The family needs my income."

"The Lord will provide whether you have a job or not. He wouldn't give me all these little children to take care of and not provide for them, or us. If He wants Palo to attend college, Palo will be given the means to do so whether you have a position or not." Mama gestured for Aria to take a sip. "Life is always easier to face with a cup of hot coffee and bread to bolster our strength," she said, dunking her bread into the steaming cup.

Aria followed suit. "How can you be sure He will provide?"

"The Bible says in Matthew chapter six, 'Behold the fowls of the air: for they sow not, neither do they reap, nor gather into barns; yet your heavenly Father feedeth them. Are ye not much better than they?' The Lord has provided for us all these years, so why would He stop now?"

Her mother paused, her finger tracing

the rim of her cup, a faraway look in her eyes. "When your father was fired, it was hard for me to adjust. I asked why God would allow a father of six to be laid off from a wonderful position that would permit our children to attend a good school and then make him a desk clerk at a struggling office where we can barely make ends meet. But every month ends *do* meet, and we even have money left over to bake fig cookies for the neighborhood children." Mama smiled. "He will always provide for His children, but it may not be in the manner we wish."

"But wasn't He providing for us through my position? Why did I have to lose it?" Once again, despair threatened to engulf Aria.

"It may not be clear now or ever, but take comfort in this, the Lord has your future and our family's future in His hands," Mama said, cupping Aria's face. "My little songbird. He treasures you far more than the birds of the air. Trust that He knows what is best."

"He treasures you far more than the birds of

the air." Mama's words echoed through Aria's mind, bathing her in peace. *All this time, I've been acting as if I am the provider when it's You, Lord. It's only ever been You.* She bowed her head. *I give You this burden, Lord, a burden that I took. I know You will provide. Someday. Somehow. You will.* "Thank you, Mama," she whispered.

"I don't want you to catch your death, so why don't you go change and I'll make you a proper breakfast?" She bent and kissed Aria's cheek.

Aria nodded and, taking her cup with her, climbed the stairs to the third floor to her old bedroom that she shared with her four sisters. Before she stripped off her soiled dress, she stepped to the curtain to draw it for a bit of privacy and thought she spied a familiar figure below gazing up at her apartment building.

"Is that Byron?" she thought out loud, nearly pressing her face into the glass to get a better look. Her motion drew the figure's gaze, but she couldn't discern his identity through the rain. When he turned away without acknowledging her, she drew the curtain, dismissing her first impression as wishful thinking. If Palo was to be released from prison, it would be through divine intervention.

CHAPTER TEN

Aria hung up the last of her freshly laundered dresses in the shared closet. After having a room to herself for so long, it felt quite crowded sleeping with her four sisters in one room. She turned to the floor-length window and gazed out onto St. Ann Street below and across to Jackson Square. She smiled as she watched her little sisters play on the green, dodging the fine folks parading about. Spying a couple with a young lady in a dowdy gray dress trailing behind them, she sighed and turned away, missing being a companion. It had only been three days since she had acted as a witness for Mildred and Mr. Branson's marriage, but those days felt like a lifetime while she waited for some word from Byron about Palo. Now that she had lost her position, she had even less money for a lawyer should Byron change his mind.

Aria bit her lip, trying not to worry about how she would help support her family now that she was unemployed and didn't have a reference for all her years of work. Tapping her chin, she thought maybe she could inquire after some of Millie's old friends and see if a younger sister needed a companion. *Whatever happens, I know You are in control, Lord.*

"Aria!" her mother called from the second floor, no doubt needing help preparing dinner.

She let the shabby curtain drop. "Coming, Mama," she called back, tying her apron over her powder-blue gown and making her way down to the kitchen area. "Where shall I start?"

"A gentleman is here to see you." Mama grinned, wiping her hands on her apron, leaving red streaks from the sauce she was preparing.

"Who?" Aria's breath caught.

"I think you know." Mama winked.

Aria stepped down the stairs with her skirts trailing behind her as her clammy hand stuck to the curved wooden stair rail. Peering through the glass of the worn french doors, she spied him waiting in the shared courtyard with his hands behind his back, staring up at the clotheslines crisscrossing from the upper levels, underclothes fluttering in the gentle breeze.

She grimaced as she smoothed her hair, wishing she hadn't worn it in a simple braid, but there was no time to fix it now. She took a deep breath and opened the door with a creak.

He turned toward her, the wrinkle in his brow easing as he caught sight of her. "Aria." His breath caught.

Her heart stopped at the sound of her name on his lips. The world around her quieted, and for a moment, nothing else existed as she stepped toward him, longing for more but not daring to hope. "Mr. Roderick." She dipped into a curtsy. "How did you know where to find me?"

"I was worried when you didn't show up at the coffeehouse, so I went to Beaumont Manor, only to find that you had been sent away." His hands traced the perimeter of his hat.

She felt the heat rise from her neck to her cheeks at the knowledge that he knew of her shameful dismissal. "I'm so sorry I kept you waiting for me at the coffeehouse. I would have sent you a note, but everything happened so fast and before I knew it, I was on the train to New Orleans with Millie and Mr. Branson and it was too late."

"So, you *were* with her." His lips pressed into a grim line. "Good. I feared the worst when I heard that she had run off with that rogue."

Aria nodded slowly, determining the soreness of the topic. "Millie made certain I arrived in New Orleans safe and sound and in turn, I made certain she was good and married before I left her in Mr. Branson's care." She looked down at her hands. "I'm sorry if you're disappointed to hear that she is married."

"I'm not sorry in the least. In fact. . ." He

took a step toward her, close enough that she could close the distance between them with a kiss if she wished. "I was going to speak with her and her father to let them know of my intent to break off the courtship."

"Oh?" She swallowed, trying not to focus on his lips. "And did you?"

"Yes. You see, I found myself in love with someone else," he whispered, tucking a wisp of hair behind her ear.

"Oh." Her heart lodged in her throat, and she had difficulty breathing.

"Now, I believe we had something to discuss," he said, dropping his hand and breaking her trance. "Your brother."

"You've seen him?" She pressed her hand to her heart.

He nodded. "Once I saw that you were safely home, I went to speak with him."

So that was him in the rain.

"And afterward, I did some investigation and found pretty indisputable evidence that your brother was not the one who stole from Brooks and Brooks." He grinned.

"Is it enough to get him released?" she asked breathlessly.

"I'd say so." Palo sauntered into the courtyard, hands in his pockets.

Aria squealed and ran to him, throwing her arms around his hard shoulders and pressing a kiss onto his bristly cheek. "Palo, thank the Lord! What happened?" She swiveled around to Byron and back to Palo.

"Mr. Roderick said he suspected the son of the shopkeeper was being underhanded, so he went all Sherlock Holmes on him!"

"Mr. Holmes, eh?" She turned to Byron, unable to stifle her grin.

Byron shrugged and returned her smile. "I merely visited every pawnshop in town until I found the watch described and discovered who pawned it."

She laughed. "You're jesting. The thief didn't use a pseudonym?"

He shook his head and chuckled. "Not very bright, that lad. I presented my findings to the elder Brooks, and all charges have been dropped. Your brother is a free man. If he does well on his entrance exams, he should have no problem getting accepted into Louisiana State University."

"I don't know how to thank you." Aria lifted her hands, unable to express all that was in her heart.

He waved her off. "I should be thanking you. Your brother's case has pushed me to finally commit to my plan of opening my own law practice in the French Quarter where I can be more useful."

"Here?" She couldn't stop the smile that flooded her face. "We will be neighbors."

"More than that, I hope," he replied so quietly that she wondered if she had heard him correctly.

He looked over her shoulder and smiled at the little faces pressed against the wavy windowpanes of the french doors.

"Come on out. We have a surprise for you," she called to them, motioning her little nieces and nephews outside. At Palo's greeting, they came tumbling out into the courtyard, bombarding their uncle with embraces and questions. "With Palo's return, you will be a hero in the family's eyes." Aria smiled up to him, wishing again she could thank him, but any words felt inadequate.

"I'm glad I could help," he replied, his smile seeming only for her.

"Would you like to come up?" Aria managed to ask over the din.

"I'd love to, but how about we take a stroll first?" He offered her his arm as the children ushered Palo inside and Mama let out a cry that could be heard for miles.

As they walked, Aria's secret burned within her, and she longed for the truth to step into the light. *I could tell him now. I have no job to lose.* She looked at him out of the corner of her eye, admiring his broad shoulders, his confident stride, and prayed her lies would not take him from her.

Byron halted alongside the Mississippi River, the scent of the muddy water wafting up to them. He bent down, picked up a pebble, and tossed it into the river, the water swallowing it without a skip.

Taking a deep breath, she began to pour out the secrets she had kept hidden in the dark. "Mr. Roderick—"

"Please, call me Byron."

"Byron," she said, loving how perfect his name felt on her lips even amid her admission, "I have a confession to make."

"Before you say anything, I need to make a confession of my own." He turned to her, taking her small hands in his. His pale hand stood out against her olive skin. "I must confess that you captured my heart the moment I first beheld you, and every moment I've spent with you afterward has only confirmed your kind, unselfish nature."

She thought back to their collision in the garden. He had not seemed all that enchanted with her as he raced away. She stepped back from him, trying to clear her head. "I'm not as wholesome as all that. You see, I deceived you." She nearly choked as she rushed onward to explain. "Granted, I was forced into the situation by my employer, but that was no excuse for allowing you to continue to believe it was Millie you met that first night." She lifted her lashes and met his gaze. "I was the masked lady." At his silence, she grasped his sleeve. "Please, can you ever forgive me for the masquerade?"

"I knew you had a good reason for why you were pretending to be Miss Beaumont."

"You knew?" She blinked, confused. "Then why. . .for how long?"

He grinned. "Ever since I spied you singing behind Millie and I gave you that Italian pastry at the musicale. No woman other than my lady from the masquerade ball would consume a sweet like that." Kneeling, he took her hand in his. "Aria St. Angelo, will you do me the honor of becoming my wife?"

For her answer, she took a seat on his knee, wrapped her arms about his neck, and pulling him into an embrace, pressed her lips to his again and again.

Grace Hitchcock is the award-winning author of multiple historical novels and novellas, including the American Royalty, Best Laid Plans, and Aprons & Veils series. She holds a Master's in Creative Writing and a Bachelor of Arts in English with a minor in History. Grace lives in South Louisiana with her husband, Dakota, sons, and daughter in a farmhouse that is always filled with the sounds of sweet little footsteps running at full speed. When not writing, chasing her toddlers, or tending to her chickens and golden and labrador retrievers, she's baking something delightful and can usually be found with a book clutched in her fist.

Sign Up for Grace's Newsletter!

Keep up to date with Grace's news on book releases and giveaways by signing up for her email list at GraceHitchcock.com

FREE from Grace Hitchcock

New Orleans, 1895

Colette Olivier, a young widow who married out of obligation, finds herself at the end of her mourning period and besieged with suitors out for her inheritance. With her pick of any man, she is drawn to an unlikely choice.

The Widow of St. Charles Avenue by Grace Hitchcock
a Second Chance Brides Novella
GraceHitchcock.com

Scan to Claim Your FREE Novella

More in your favorite series . . .

With a hope for belonging, Belle Parish leaves her position as a maid in Charleston to travel to New Mexico to become a mail-order bride. Colt Lawson's letters hold great promise, but something does not add up. Belle flees straight into the Castañeda Hotel Harvey House. Giving up the prospect of marrying, she focuses on her role as a Harvey Girl waitress until a strong Texas Ranger rides into her life.

The Pursuit of Miss Parish by Grace Hitchcock
Aprons & Veils #2
A Mail-Order Bride RomCom

Of all the dares Lorna Elliot had accepted, becoming a Harvey Girl waitress was by far the dumbest. And she had done it to herself in a fit of pique over a Texas Ranger who was mooning over another woman, but now that Ranger Reid is the new sheriff in her hometown, it's going to be impossible for her to move on unless she takes control of her heart—for better, or for worse.

The Enchanting of Miss Elliot by Grace Hitchcock
Aprons & Veils #3
A Friends-to-Lovers RomCom

Tanner Sterling has hunted his last bounty. As a new foreman, he wasn't expecting to rescue a sweet Harvey Girl from a raging river his first day. But, when he sees her on a wanted poster, he knows hunters will be coming for her. Despite wanting to hang up his past along with his gun belt, Tanner will do anything to protect her from the coming storm . . . even if he has to claim the bounty himself.

The Vanishing of Miss Victoria by Grace Hitchcock
Aprons & Veils #4
An Enemies-to-Lovers RomCom

www.ingramcontent.com/pod-product-compliance
Lightning Source LLC
LaVergne TN
LVHW091000080826
845145LV00003B/1072

* 9 7 8 1 9 7 0 6 7 5 0 5 4 *